THE LIFE & DEATH OF CODY PARKER

A TANNER NOVEL - BOOK 5

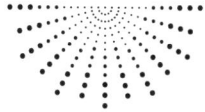

REMINGTON KANE

INTRODUCTION

THE LIFE & DEATH OF CODY PARKER – TANNER BOOK 5

In the town of Stark, Texas, Tanner faces ghosts from his past as he tries to keep history from repeating itself.

ACKNOWLEDGMENTS

I write for you.

—Remington Kane

1

KING OF THE ROAD

Forty hours after he leapt off a pedestrian walkway and onto a train, Tanner awoke to find himself still riding the rails. He was also fighting for his life, as a large man lifted him from the floor and slammed him against a wall of the train car.

Tanner, still weak from his wounds, slid to the floor and let out a moan. The moan was real, as was the pain that gave it birth, but he exaggerated his reaction and let his hands drop onto his lap.

The behemoth who had assaulted Tanner glared down at him in disgust, then started in on an old man who was cowering in a corner.

"I want everything you two got, otherwise, I'll toss you off the train."

The man had a long black beard that nearly covered his entire face, leaving just a potato-size nose and two dark eyes showing.

Tanner made his move as the brute reached for the old man. He sent an uppercut between the big man's legs to smash his testicles. The brute bent over so fast that he slammed the crown of his head against the wall beside the old man and suffered a cut from the impact.

Tanner had given the punch everything he had, but because he was weakened from the gunshot wound he'd recently suffered, it was a question of who would recover first, him or the big man.

It was Tanner who recovered first. He jabbed stiff fingers at the man's throat, but the blow was cushioned by the woolly beard and had little effect.

Then Tanner watched with surprise as the old man kicked the big man in the gut and sent him tumbling backwards.

Tanner grabbed the brute by his beard and dragged him toward the open door of the moving train car, with the intention of pushing him off. The man realized what he planned to do, and in a panic, he made it to his feet.

Tanner let go of the beard, tried to hit him in the throat again and managed only to jab the man on the ear.

The bearded man growled and reached out a hand to grab Tanner's throat, but Tanner ducked beneath the man's outstretched arm and rammed his clenched fists into the bully's gut. The man bellowed in fear as he nearly fell from the moving car, but he managed to snag the edge of the door with his right hand.

Unfortunately for him, his weight caused the door to slide shut, while most of his body was still leaning outside the train.

Once the door slammed into his left foot, which was supporting his weight, his fate was decided. He tumbled out of the train car with a scream on his lips, as the door slammed shut behind him.

The old man came over and slid open the door to peer back down the tracks. "Ouch! That tumble will have him spending time in a hospital for sure."

When the old man looked back at Tanner, he saw that he was down on one knee.

"You're dizzy, aren't you? Well, that's no surprise after the fever you've had."

Tanner stood on weak legs, walked over to the back wall, and slid down to a sitting position with his legs straight out in front of him. The old man brought him a bottle of water that was half-filled, and Tanner drained it.

Tanner stared at the old man and found that he had vague memories concerning him.

"You helped me, didn't you?"

"I got that bullet out of you."

Tanner nodded, as the events of the last two days came back to him.

AFTER LEAVING RIDGE CREEK, HE HAD EVADED BEING captured by leaping into a moving coal car, which passed within feet of the train car full of sand he'd first leapt into. By the time that second train finally came to a stop, he found himself in Bowling Green, Kentucky, with a throat as dry as the sand he once laid upon.

Judging by the position of the sun, it was mid-morning. Tanner realized he must have slept for hours. He had a fever to go with the dry throat. After checking the wound in his chest, he knew it needed tending to or it would become infected, if it hadn't already done so.

There was construction going on at the train depot in Kentucky. Inside the job trailer of a plumbing contractor Tanner found bottled water and a first aid kit, along with a bag of potato chips.

After gobbling down the chips, he went through the

two desks in the office and found a pint of whisky, along with a prescription bottle with eight pills remaining inside.

The pills were white, oval-shaped and labeled as cephalexin, an antibiotic usually prescribed for upper respiratory infections. According to the date on the pharmacy label, the pills had likely expired. However, thieves, like beggars, can't be choosers.

After cleaning his wound with the whisky, Tanner downed two of the pills and pocketed the bottle, then he considered finding somewhere on the property to rest up.

It was not to be. The office had a window in the wall, and through it, Tanner had seen a man wearing sunglasses talking to two cops who were inside a patrol car. The man with the sunglasses was pointing toward the trailer he was in.

The man must have seen him enter the trailer, which had been locked and pried open by Tanner using a claw hammer he'd found nearby.

Tanner had stuffed the bandages and painkillers from the first aid kit into a pocket of his cargo pants. It was as he was doing that, he realized he no longer had the gun he had used in Ridge Creek, the one which had been the chief of police's duty weapon.

The empty gun had been tucked in his waistband, but it must have fallen out along the way; Tanner's best guess is that it was still in the train car that carried the coal.

Acquiring a new weapon would have to wait, and Tanner left the trailer before the cops could trap him inside. He'd made it clear of the trailer, but when more cops joined the hunt, Tanner again climbed aboard a train car, riding inside for once, and traveled toward who knew where.

The train just kept rolling, and as it did, Tanner felt himself become more feverish. He swallowed more of the antibiotics but doubted they would work any better than the first dose had.

In time, he slept, but awoke to see an old man peering down at him with a concerned expression. He knew the man was old because he glimpsed the deep wrinkles around the man's eyes, but he could see little detail in the gloom of the darkened train car.

"That bullet must come out," the old man said, and Tanner had nodded in agreement.

"Where are we?"

"Just outside Dallas."

"Texas?"

"Yeah."

The old man had held a bottle of water to his lips and Tanner drank it greedily, while realizing how weak he had grown. He knew he was hot with fever. He also realized that it was night again and had a vague memory of stumbling out of one train car and climbing into another.

"Doctor," he said.

The old man smiled. "Just call me, Doc."

And then Tanner was out again.

The next time he opened his eyes was when he was rudely awakened by the bearded man he had shoved off the train.

TANNER STOOD AND FELT THE PAIN IN HIS WOUND. WHEN he looked at it, he saw it had been bandaged. He lifted the bloodstained gauze that had been taped in place and found a neat row of blue stitches that appeared to be made of simple sewing thread. He looked down at the old man, who was seated on the floor of the train car.

"You do decent work."

"Thank you. And you're not the first man I've had to stitch up on the fly."

Tanner's clothes were damp with sweat and he smelled sour, but when he laid a hand on his forehead, he could tell that the fever had broken. He looked out through the open door and saw desert, but he could also make out a highway in the distance.

When his bladder reminded him there were more urgent matters than sightseeing, Tanner stood at the edge of the open door, whipped it out, and watched his stream wet the weeds that grew between his train and the tracks on the opposite side.

"Where are we?"

The old man pointed toward the south. "We should be pulling into the train yard at Culver, Texas, in about twenty minutes."

Tanner turned his head and blinked at the old man, as surprise animated his usually stoic features.

"Culver?"

"Yeah, there's not much there but the train yard, but to the east is the town of—"

"Stark," Tanner said. "To the east is Stark, Texas."

"I guess you've been there before, because Stark is barely a dot on the map."

Tanner nodded. "Yeah, I've been there before," he said, and his mind drifted off into memory.

2
CODY PARKER

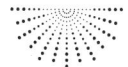

STARK, TEXAS, SEPTEMBER 1997

THE YOUNG MAN WITH THE TRIM BEARD CALLING HIMSELF Tanner had stopped on the side of the road to consult a map. That was when he spotted a dog being chased across a field by three coyotes.

The dog was a beagle; his short legs were no match for the predators who pursued him. Tanner guessed that the coyotes would catch up to the dog within seconds.

When something on the dog's neck twinkled, Tanner assumed it was a license or name tag attached to a collar. That meant that the hound was someone's pet. He thought about trying to shoot the beasts pursuing it, but his gun lacked the range and would be useless.

Four seconds later, the fastest of the coyotes moved within inches of the dog. That was when Tanner saw the creature's head explode. He heard the first rifle shot, then watched the other two coyotes be torn apart by gunfire, followed by the echo of two more blasts.

Tanner looked over toward the right where a man held a rifle steady. It was perched on the top horizontal slat of a white fence and at least a hundred yards away. The man had hit three running targets with consecutive shots from that distance, a feat that Tanner would find difficult to duplicate.

When the man sprang over the fence and began walking toward the quivering hound he had saved, Tanner tossed the map back in his car and went out to meet him. Tanner was closer to the dog, so he was closer to the dead coyotes as well. When he checked the bodies, he saw that all three had been put down by head wounds.

"Damn impressive," Tanner muttered. He became further impressed as the man drew closer and he saw that the marksman was even younger than he was. The kid was probably no more than sixteen or seventeen, with dark hair peeking out from beneath the cowboy hat he wore.

At least, he looked young if you didn't consider the boy's eyes, which broadcast more experience than they should have.

"That was some damn fine shooting, kid."

The boy glanced at him and Tanner could tell that the kid had spotted the bulge of the gun on his hip, beneath his untucked shirt.

After giving a loud whistle for the dog, the animal came over to the boy and rubbed against his legs, while still shaking from fright.

When the boy slung the rifle onto his back by its strap, Tanner could see that it was a Remington 760 with a scope. The pump-action rifle was older than the kid, since they stopped making them some time ago, although the one across the kid's back looked to be in good shape.

After squatting down to pet the dog, the boy looked up at Tanner.

"Are you passing through, mister?"

"More or less, but maybe you can help me. I'm looking for the McKay Ranch."

The boy stood again, and Tanner realized he was almost his height and over six feet tall.

After looking Tanner over again, the boy asked a question. "What kind of work is McKay paying you to do?"

"Well, that would be between him and me, wouldn't it?"

The boy just stared at him. So intense was his gaze that Tanner felt the weight of it as he stared back. The boy broke eye contact and pointed down the road in the direction that Tanner's car was facing.

"Go another three miles and you'll be on McKay's land."

Tanner nodded his thanks, then turned to walk back to his car. As he did so, he spoke over his shoulder. "What's your name, kid?"

"I'm Cody Parker, what's yours?"

"Call me Tanner."

"Hey, Tanner."

Tanner stopped walking and turned back to look at the boy. "Yeah?"

"I'm not a kid."

Tanner smiled. It was only several years earlier that he was the boy's age. He remembered that he hated being called a kid too. It was the main reason he grew the beard.

"I'll remember that, Cody, and maybe I'll see you around."

Cody Parker tipped his hat and walked off with the dog at his side.

Tanner took one more look at the bodies of the three coyotes and nodded his head slightly.

"Damn fine shooting," he muttered, then he headed for his meeting with Andy McKay.

3

THE OLD AND THE NEW

While seated, Tanner checked the pockets of the cargo pants he was wearing and felt the money he had placed inside one of them. It was a little less than five thousand dollars. He looked over at the old man and saw him smile.

"That's quite a bundle of cash you've got there."

"You went through my pockets?"

"Yeah, and if I hadn't, I wouldn't have found those antibiotics you had on you. Those pills saved your life, you know? I think it was just enough to fight off the fever and infection you had."

Tanner touched his wound. "You took the bullet out and stitched me up inside a moving train car?"

"I sure did. I keep a needle and thread in my pack. And lucky for you the bullet wasn't too deep and hit nothing vital."

Tanner counted out two thousand dollars and passed it to the old man, whose eyes bulged at the sight of so much cash headed his way.

"That's payment for helping me."

"Damn, son. I haven't seen this much cash at one time in years."

"What's your name?"

"You can call me Doc."

"Are you a doctor?"

"I was, but that was many years ago. Now I'm just an old man making it day by day."

"Why didn't you call the police when you realized I'd been shot? That way, you could have also taken my money."

The old man chuckled. "I hate the damn cops. All they ever do is hassle you. And you look like a man who would hold a grudge and come looking for me someday."

Tanner thought about pointing out that, given how sick he had been with the fever, the old man could have easily murdered him and taken the money.

The fact that some people never considered killing someone, no matter how expedient it would be, always puzzled Tanner. He had never had a problem with killing anyone if he thought it the best course of action. But then, his conscience, his sense of right and wrong, had always differed from that of others.

"What's this depot like? Will there be heavy security there?"

"Maybe, but I doubt it. A train yard is like everywhere else these days, fewer people doing more work. Most of the time, the guards stay in their shack and keep out of the sun. Besides, I know how to avoid the cameras."

"I need a place to wash up."

"There's a truck stop a mile from the depot, you can even shower there."

Tanner studied the old man. "Why were you headed to Stark, Texas?"

"I heard there was work. I can't do much at my age,

but I can still muck out a stall. Of course, thanks to you, I no longer need the money."

"One of the ranches is hiring?"

"Yeah, the Reyes Ranch, a Mexican family owns it."

Tanner looked out at the passing scenery and spotted the highway in the distance.

"That's Highway 16, isn't it?"

"Yeah and the ranch is not far from it."

"Are you from this area?"

Doc nodded. "Originally, yeah."

"The Reyes Ranch, what did it used to be called?"

The old man's back straightened. "Oh, so you know about that, huh? Yeah, it's the same ranch. The Reyes Ranch used to be called the Parker Ranch, and after the… tragedy, I guess you might call it, the place just sat there for years."

Tanner stared at the old man. "Tragedy? That's one way of putting it."

The old man squinted at Tanner. "Were you around here back then?"

Tanner ignored the question and stood as the train began to slow. "Show me where this truck stop is, and after that… I guess I'll go to the ranch with you."

Doc smiled. "Fine, I could use the company."

They left the train yard without being harassed and walked across the wide sandy field that separated them from the highway.

The old man wrinkled his nose as the breeze carried Tanner's scent.

"You're a bit ripe, son, fever will do that. They sell a little clothing at the truck stop too, nothing fancy, but you might consider getting new clothes before you shower."

Tanner looked down at the black shirt he was wearing.

It was ripped and bloody, and he could smell the stink coming off it as well.

"New clothes sound like a good idea."

"I'll also change that bandage for you. But say, how did you get shot?"

Tanner smirked. "I underestimated a very devious woman."

"Your wife?"

"No, and tell me something, this store inside the truck stop, do they sell phones?"

"I don't know, but the last time I was here, they still had a pay phone."

"Good, I need to make a call."

"Say son, what's your name?"

Tanner thought for a moment, as he tried to recall one of the fake names he'd chosen, but he had burned through so many of them recently that he decided to just use the one that had been handed down to him by his mentor.

"I'm Tanner."

"Well, Tanner, I hear the ranch is hiring security. Judging by the way you handled that dude on the train, I'd say they'll hire you on."

"Why would they need security?"

"The story I heard is that some local big shot is hassling them."

"That sounds familiar."

Doc stopped walking. "You're thinking about what happened back when it was the Parker Ranch, but don't worry, the way I hear it, this thing isn't that serious."

"Has the law gotten involved?"

"Maybe, but I don't know much about it."

∽

THE HIGHWAY 16 TRUCK STOP TURNED OUT TO BE A massive complex that housed a restaurant, offered truck repair, and had a shop where Tanner outfitted himself in a new pair of jeans and a black T-shirt.

The store also sold cheap cell phones. After showering and getting his bandage changed by Doc, Tanner stepped outside and made a call.

After eight rings, a cautious voice answered. "Hello?"

"Tim, it's me, Tanner."

"Oh, thank God. Madison and I were worried about you. The newspaper in Ridge Creek wrote a story that said you'd been shot. What happened?"

Tanner gave Tim Jackson a quick explanation of what had occurred over the last few days, including the events in Ridge Creek.

"I guess the farm is burned now that the FBI is looking at it?" Tim said.

"No, I have an idea about that, but I'll need you to find someone."

Tanner told Tim what he wanted to do, and Tim said he would handle it.

"I'll find him, but are you certain he'll do it?"

"No, I'm not sure. But once you find him, get a number where I can call him."

"I will, and I'll send out those materials you want too."

"The sooner the better," Tanner said, as the "materials" Tim mentioned, were Tanner's newest fake ID.

After talking to Tim, Tanner joined Doc at a booth inside the restaurant. As he ate, Tanner felt his strength returning. He downed three glasses of orange juice with his meal as well, as the fever had left him dehydrated.

Along with the bandaged gunshot wound, Tanner also wore a wrapping of gauze around his midsection, as his leap into the train had injured the ribs on his left side. He had also been wounded on his right leg, but the bullet that caused it had barely touched him and left behind only a purple bruise.

Once he finished eating, Tanner leaned back and asked Doc what he knew about the town of Stark, Texas.

Doc stifled a burp and began talking. "After the... thing out at the Parker Ranch, the town started to die. The Parkers were gone, but so was McKay, and between the two of them, they employed a lot of men. Without that revenue, the town shriveled up."

Tanner pointed out the window beside their booth. "That's Stark over there in the distance, and I see three tall buildings that weren't there years ago, so I guess the town made a comeback."

"It sure did, and you can thank a dude named Chuck Willis for that. He came here from San Antonio, bought up the McKay land and started building an office complex. It's a huge place, like a college campus. And along with it, he built the housing so that his employees would have someplace to live."

"Why didn't Willis buy the Parker Ranch too?"

"He was too late. Reyes had already bought it cheap and started breeding horses."

"Horses? No cattle?"

"The cattle business dried up around here. Reyes, whoever he is, must be doing well breeding horses, because he's refused to sell his land to Willis."

"But Willis doesn't take no for an answer. Is that why Reyes is hiring security?"

"What I heard is that a horse was poisoned and nearly died. They raise quarter horses, racehorses, and those animals can be worth a pretty penny. Plus, some of the ranch hands got hurt in accidents. The thing is, though, the accidents weren't accidents. The story I heard is that one guy fell from a ladder that had a top rung sawn through. He broke his arm in the fall."

They left the truck stop and walked across more desert scrubland, as they headed toward the town of Stark, Texas.

As they drew closer, Tanner's mind again filled with memories.

4
INDECENT PROPOSAL

STARK, TEXAS, SEPTEMBER 1997

Tanner was escorted into Andy McKay's office.

The large room was masculine in every aspect, from its wood paneling to the genuine bearskin rug that covered the floor in the center of the room.

A large wooden desk sat before a wide window that looked out on a green pasture, upon which a score of cattle could be seen grazing in the distance. A console TV sat in one corner of the room by the door, while a smaller desk was in the opposite corner and had a computer sitting atop it.

The computer was one of many Tanner had seen inside a home recently. He thought that the machines were rapidly gaining in popularity, although he himself had never used one. That would change, as he was always ready to learn a new skill.

The man who escorted Tanner into the office was tall but had a gut that made him look fat. Tanner could tell the man believed his girth and height made him intimidating. He was also aware that the man didn't like him, and believed he knew why. McKay was bringing Tanner in to handle a problem that the fat man thought he could do himself and the man felt resentful.

The man had told Tanner that his name was Jack Sheer, right before asking Tanner how old he was. Sheer was in his forties and no doubt thought that anyone under thirty wasn't worth a damn. Tanner didn't care what Sheer thought. He just wanted to know who McKay wanted dead, so he could do the job and head back to Dallas.

Despite having grown up in a succession of rural environments, Tanner liked cities, and he wanted to leave Stark as soon as possible.

From behind his massive wooden desk, McKay studied Tanner as the hit man walked in and took a seat. Tanner guessed that McKay was in his early fifties and could see that the lean man was in good condition. Judging by the stern expression on his face, McKay was a man who took things seriously.

McKay was graying at the temples, and his lined and sun-browned skin told Tanner that McKay spent more time outdoors than inside the office. After reaching across the desk to shake hands, McKay told Jack Sheer to close the door on his way out.

Sheer hesitated to leave. "Don't you want me to sit in, Andy?"

"No, but go see to that other matter we talked about."

"I got Dave and his brother handling that."

"I want you to handle it; it has to be done right."

"All right, I'll go see to that," Sheer said, and then Tanner was alone with Andy McKay.

McKay looked Tanner over. "You're younger than I'd thought you'd be."

"Why is that?"

"I heard about you from two men; one was Robertson, the man that sent you here. But there's another fella I know real well who said he hired you once, only that couldn't be you, because the man named Tanner that he hired was older, and that was ten years ago."

"That man your friend hired was my mentor; when he died, I took the name Tanner, just like he did when his mentor died."

"What's your real name?"

"Does it matter?"

"I guess not, but I hope you're the man I need, because what I want done will take guts and it's… complicated."

"You want someone dead or I wouldn't be here. Tell me who it is and why you want them dead. If I agree to take the job, I'll kill them. It's just that simple."

"What if I want you to kill more than one?"

"I'm sure that Robertson told you my price, just multiply that and you have my fee."

McKay took a deep breath, let it out slowly, and leaned across the desk.

"Here's the thing…"

∼

LESS THAN A MINUTE LATER, TANNER WAS OUT OF HIS SEAT and headed for the office door. McKay left his desk and trailed behind him.

"I thought you were a professional, Tanner. Why won't you take the job?"

"I gave you my answer, McKay. Go find somebody else. It shouldn't be hard to do; the world is full of maniacs."

Tanner stopped to open the door and McKay spun him around.

"I thought you were supposed to be a stone-cold killer, but you're just a boy still, aren't you?"

"My age has nothing to do with it. I'm a killer, yes, but not a butcher or a madman. Listen to me, if you go through with what you want, the law will pin it on you. Hiring outside help won't stop them from tracing it back to you."

McKay looked him up and down, as disgust covered his face. "You're just a gutless punk."

Tanner opened the door. "Goodbye, McKay. Forget that we met."

Tanner strode down a hall to the front door, where he went down porch steps and into the wide driveway, while looking for signs of trouble. Then he was in his car and driving toward the graveled path that would take him back to the county road.

INSIDE THE RANCH HOUSE, MCKAY GRABBED A WALKIE-talkie from off a table. "Jack, come in."

There was the sound of static, followed by Jack Sheer's voice. "What's up, Andy?"

"Tanner is headed your way. You boys kill that son of a bitch and I'll give you two grand each."

"You got it."

AFTER ROUNDING A CURVE ON THE GRAVELED DRIVE THAT connected McKay's ranch to the road, Tanner stopped the car and stepped out into the hot afternoon sun. He had refused to kill for McKay because what the man wanted done was madness. Insane or not, McKay wasn't stupid. Tanner knew he would not be allowed to just ride away once he knew McKay's plans.

That "other matter" of which McKay had spoken about to Jack Sheer was no doubt an ambush. The driveway was lined on both sides by jacaranda trees that were still in bloom with their purple flowers, and beyond them was white fencing, followed by flat arid land. However, the road leading out of the ranch curved in both directions from where Tanner stopped the car and it placed him out of the line of sight.

If he attempted to drive off, he'd be shot to death inside the car, and if he tried to run away, there would be no way to avoid being spotted on the flat terrain.

The car itself was of no concern, because he had stolen it just for the meeting, knowing that negotiations sometimes went awry with a new client, and that his transportation might need to be abandoned.

Tanner got into position and waited for McKay's men to grow impatient and come to him.

JACK SHEER CAME AROUND THE BEND FIRST WITH TWO MEN following behind, and all three men were armed. Sheer had a sawed-off shotgun in one hand and a walkie-talkie in the other. Tanner could hear McKay's voice sounding tinny and weak, as it came from the speaker of the walkie-talkie.

"He must be inside the car, blast it."

A second passed, and then the quiet day erupted into the thunderous sound of multiple weapons firing, as Sheer and the men with him blasted Tanner's car, shredding the seats, destroying the dash, and shattering all the windows.

The barrage was brutal but short-lived, as first Sheer and then the two men with him fell onto the gravel with wounds to their feet.

When all three men were down and moaning in agony, Tanner slid out from beneath the car and went for their weapons.

The two men with Sheer were too concerned with their wounds to think about the revolvers they'd dropped, but Jack Sheer reached out to grab his shotgun, and Tanner shot him in the foot again.

That finished Sheer, who rolled over onto his back and began crying from the pain, as blood formed in a puddle around his foot.

Tanner tossed the two revolvers away but kept the shotgun, then he picked up the walkie-talkie.

"McKay."

There was a pause, but then McKay spoke. "Tanner?"

"Forget your plans. And if you come after me again, I'll kill you."

There was no answer. Tanner dropped the unit and stomped it with the heel of his boot. After rounding the curve, he came across the pickup truck that Sheer and his men had used to block the driveway. Tanner got in it and drove off to see Frank Parker.

5
ENTRANCE EXAM

Tanner and Doc walked along a county road that was wider than Tanner remembered it being.

It had been a two-lane road mostly used by ranchers, but was now a four-lane thoroughfare, which Doc told Tanner had been extended, and ended at a ramp that would place you on Highway 16.

"That sounds much quicker than taking Derby Street to Culver Avenue," Tanner said, and Doc gave him a strange look.

"You said you hadn't been here for years, but you remember the street names. Either you've got a great memory, or you've spent a good deal of time here."

Tanner looked over at Doc but didn't comment. A moment later, something ahead caught their attention.

There was a pickup truck blocking the entrance to the Reyes Ranch. Two toughs were getting out of it and looking their way.

Doc gestured at them. "What do you think? Are they trouble? Or maybe Reyes already hired security."

"We'll soon find out," Tanner said.

As they drew closer, Tanner could tell that the two men were related, likely brothers. Both were watching them with interest.

It was a hot day, and yet, the men wore unbuttoned denim shirts over their white tees. The shirts were there to cover their guns, which judging by the outlines Tanner could discern, were just jammed in their waistbands, and not sheathed in holsters.

The men were both about forty and had dull eyes set in slack faces. The one on the right had hair two shades darker than the man on the left, but other than that they looked like twins. They reminded Tanner of Earl and Merle Carter, except these boys were meaner looking and twice the size of Merle and Earl.

Doc smiled at the men. "Howdy boys. How's it going?"

The one with the darker hair walked over and stared at them. Tanner guessed he was at least six foot five.

"If you two are headed to the Reyes Ranch, you can just turn around."

"Why is that?" Tanner said.

The big man smirked. "It's because I said so."

Tanner pointed over at the entrance to the Reyes Ranch. "Is that girl with you?"

When the man turned his head to look, Tanner reached over and yanked the gun from beneath the man's shirt.

The man cried out, "Hey, don't!"

Tanner pressed the gun against the man's stomach, as his brother came walking over.

"Tell your brother to toss away his gun or I'll blow a hole in you and use you for a shield."

"What's going on, Ernie?" the man's brother asked. He couldn't see what was happening, but he could tell that something was wrong by the way his brother's posture had stiffened.

"He's got my gun, Rich, and he wants you to toss yours away."

"Shit! How did he get your gun?"

"He tricked me. But never mind that, just toss away your gun."

Rich took his gun out but didn't drop it. "It's a bluff. He won't shoot you."

Ernie looked into Tanner's eyes. "It's no bluff, this dude will shoot. Damn it, toss the gun away."

Rich hesitated for a moment, but then threw his gun into the sand on the side of the road.

Tanner spoke to Doc, who had been watching the scene with his mouth hanging open. "Go get the gun and grab that shotgun from its rack in the truck."

"What?"

"The gun, Doc; go get it. And the shotgun in the truck too."

Doc shook himself as if he were trying to wake up, but he followed Tanner's instructions, as Tanner told Ernie to join his brother. He then had both men lean back against the truck bed.

A car drove past as the drama unfolded. The driver was alone and seemed absorbed by a conversation he was having on his cell phone. The man never turned his head to look at them, or to glance into his rearview mirror.

"Who do you two work for, Chuck Willis?"

The brothers kept quiet and only glared at Tanner.

Doc recovered the gun and removed the shotgun from inside the pickup.

The guns, both .44 Magnum revolvers, had their serial numbers filed off, while the shotgun was loaded with 12-gauge buckshot.

"On your way," Tanner said, and the two bruisers climbed into their truck. Before driving away Ernie stuck his head out the window.

"We'll remember you," he told Tanner, then he drove off.

As the truck became a dot in the distance, Doc let out a long sigh. "I about peed my pants when you grabbed that gun from his waistband. I thought for sure the other one would start shooting."

"I guess now we know why Reyes is hiring security guards."

Tanner gave Doc the handguns and the old man put them in his pack, while Tanner carried the shotgun pointed downward.

They walked down a paved driveway that Tanner remembered being gravel the last time he was there, and when they came upon the house, its size surprised him.

The place was new, no more than ten years old. It was a ranch-style house that was still bigger than the two-story house the Parker home had been. It sat in the same place as the old structure. There was also a new barn and a massive stable. Although everything looked different, being back on the ranch still stirred something in Tanner.

His reverie was broken as a rider approached from the left. The woman riding the black horse stopped the beast abruptly, as she spotted the shotgun in Tanner's hand.

Tanner sat the gun on a nearby tree stump, then walked over to speak to the woman.

"Mrs. Reyes?"

Maria Reyes nodded to Tanner while taking him in, and after looking at Doc, she asked a question.

"Are you with those men parked outside?"

"No. I took their guns and sent them away."

Maria cocked her head as she studied him. She was a

beautiful Mexican American woman in her mid-forties with flawless light brown skin. She sat atop the huge stallion as if it were an extension of her.

"You took guns away from the Harvey brothers?"

"I didn't catch their last names, but they called each other Ernie and Rich."

"That's them. And what's your name?"

"I'm Tanner, and that's Doc."

Maria's eyes flowed over Tanner once more. "Are you looking for work, Mr. Tanner?"

"Yes."

Maria smiled. "Consider yourself hired."

6
FAIR WARNING

THE PARKER RANCH, SEPTEMBER 1997

Cody Parker walked into the kitchen holding the dog he had saved under one arm, just as his twin sisters were headed out the back door with their friend, an auburn-haired girl named Tonya.

All three girls were eleven years old and classmates. Tonya had been headed out the door first, but she stopped suddenly and grinned back at Cody.

"You found my dog!"

"I told you I would. Now make sure you close the gate at your house from now on."

"I will," Tonya said, as she took her dog from him and smiled dreamily. Her crush on Cody was evident to anyone with eyes.

The blonde-haired identical twins were named Jill and Jessie, and Jessie, being the bossier of the two girls, grabbed Tonya's sleeve and pulled her back toward the door with one hand, as she balanced a plate in the other. The twins were holding food and drink in the form of fried chicken, biscuits, and single-serve cartons of juice.

"Where are you going with all that food?" Cody asked. His stepmother, Claire, who was seated at the kitchen table, answered him.

"They wanted to have a picnic."

"That looks like a lot of food for three little girls."

"We'll eat it all," Jill said, and then the girls were gone.

Claire gave Cody a sour look as she spotted the rifle slung across his back. "Do you have to tote that thing with you everywhere you go?"

Cody stared at her. Claire Parker married his father, Frank Parker, less than a year earlier after discovering she was pregnant with Frank's child. At thirty, she was closer to Cody's age than that of his father, and the two of them seemed to rub each other the wrong way.

Claire was a blonde and had regained her shapely figure in a short time after giving birth to a son, James, who sat in his high chair beside her.

"I'm just placing the rifle on the porch, so I can clean it later."

"It's not loaded, is it?"

"No."

Claire sent Cody a small smile. "I just worry about the girls getting hold of it, you know?"

"Jill and Jessie know better than to play with weapons. They've got .22s of their own."

Claire had been feeding the baby, Cody's stepbrother. Cody's words caused her to lower the hand holding the spoon near the high chair.

"Those little girls own rifles?"

"They got them a year ago on Christmas. They fired them a couple of times and then lost interest."

Claire shook her head. She had grown up on the east coast in a northern state and had never been around guns while growing up.

"The girls are only eleven."

"I started shooting a lot younger than that. Is my father here?"

"He's in the living room with a visitor, a man named Tanner."

"I know Tanner. I met him earlier."

Little James made a mewing sound and smiled up at Cody.

"Aren't you going to say hello to your brother?" Claire asked.

Cody walked over and took James' small hand in his own. "He's getting bigger."

"Yes, and I think he looks like you and your father too."

"People always said that I looked like my mother," Cody said, and Claire tensed up at the mention of the first Mrs. Parker, who died when Cody was only eight.

"Um, dinner will be ready at six."

"All right, but this Tanner, do you know why he's talking to my father?"

"No, but it seemed like something serious."

~

FRANK PARKER PACED BACK AND FORTH ACROSS THE LIVING room of his home after hearing what Tanner had to say about his meeting with Andy McKay.

Parker was a handsome man with dark hair and green eyes. He appeared younger than his forty-six years. He stopped his pacing and looked at Tanner again, who was seated on a sofa.

"All of us, not just me?"

"Yes, all of you. And then he wanted this house burned to the ground."

Frank Parker settled across from Tanner by sitting on the edge of a table that sat near the windows.

"My daughters are just kids, and my son, my youngest son… he's just a baby."

"Yeah, and he was willing to pay extra for him. Mr. Parker, McKay wants every last one of you dead. What I'm wondering is why?"

Parker paced again, but then walked back to the windows and gazed out as he spoke to Tanner.

"My new wife, Claire, she and I had an affair while she was still married to McKay. We couldn't help it; we fell in love."

Tanner nodded. "That explains it. I figured it had to be personal for him to hate you so much."

"McKay and I used to be friends, good friends… until I met Claire. Still, I can't believe he would be so ruthless."

"Love changes a man, but so does hate, and while love usually fades with time, hate deepens."

Frank Parker gave a weary sigh. "I don't know what to do. The county sheriff is McKay's brother."

"That does complicate things, but there's only one way to handle this—McKay has to die. Otherwise, it's just a matter of time before he finds someone who won't turn him down."

Parker spun around. "Why did he try to hire you?"

"I was referred. I've done this sort of work before, not the craziness McKay has in mind, but I've killed for money."

Parker blinked several times at that news and broke eye contact, before asking a question.

"Would you kill McKay for me?"

"No. At this point I'd be a prime suspect. But Parker, McKay needs to die. The way I see it, it's either you and your family or it's him."

Parker walked over and stood before Tanner. "I appreciate you coming here to warn me, but I guess all I can do is hire bodyguards."

"I'll kill McKay," said a voice from the doorway.

When Tanner turned around in his seat, he saw Cody Parker walking into the room.

"You were eavesdropping," Cody's father said.

"I was listening in, and Tanner is right, McKay needs to die."

Tanner stood and walked over to stare into Cody's eyes. "You really think you could kill a man? It's not like shooting a coyote."

Cody met Tanner's gaze. "Like you said, it's him or us."

Frank Parker walked over with his hands held up. "Whoa! Nobody's killing anybody. I'll hire some bodyguards and then go talk to the man. I can reason with Andy. Like I said, we used to be friends."

Cody pointed back toward the kitchen. "McKay hates you because of that woman in there and I warned you that she was nothing but trouble."

"*That woman* is your new mother, and I've told you more than once, we didn't plan to fall in love, it just happened."

Cody shook his head at his father. "She's not my mother; she's just your wife."

Frank placed a hand on his son's shoulder. "I love her, boy."

Cody's expression softened. "I know, Dad, but loving her has turned you into a fool."

Tanner watched this exchange in fascination. The boy, Cody, seemed to be more of a man than his father was.

Parker offered Tanner his hand. "I thank you for warning me about McKay's intentions, and like I said, I'll hire bodyguards. I'll also let others know what he tried to do. That alone should stop him from going through with it. The man might want me dead, but he also doesn't want to wind up on death row."

"I wish you luck then," Tanner said.

"Why don't we hire you to be a bodyguard?" Cody said to Tanner.

"I don't do that sort of work, kid… sorry, I meant to say Cody."

Cody stared into Tanner's eyes. "I trust you. You could have taken the job, or you could have just left without saying anything. Instead, you came here to warn us. Why not see things to the end?"

Tanner smiled. He couldn't help it. He liked the kid. "I don't come cheap."

"Room and board and a thousand a month," Cody said.

"Two thousand, and it won't take a month."

"Done," Cody said.

Frank Parker was watching this exchange silently, but then he found his voice. "Hey! Who does the hiring around here, boy?"

"We need him, Dad."

"I should consult Claire."

"I'll pay him myself if I have to," Cody said, "but Tanner is staying."

Parker sighed and looked over at Tanner. "Do you believe this kid? And let me tell you, he was always like this. You'd think he was my father and not the other way around."

"He's a man all right," Tanner said, and he shook Cody's hand.

"We have a deal?" Cody asked.

Tanner gripped Cody's hand tighter. "Yes sir, Mr. Parker, we have a deal."

7

REGRETS

The barn at the Reyes Ranch was used for storage. It didn't smell as bad as Tanner thought it might.

Maria Reyes had shown Doc and Tanner the loft apartment at the top of the barn. Even though it had its own entrance on the side, it still smelled faintly like the hay that was stored beneath it. The tiny apartment had a kitchenette, bathroom, and a washer/dryer combo. It had been the ranch foreman's residence, but that man had recently married his pregnant girlfriend and bought a house.

The ranch foreman also had use of an old pickup truck until he bought a better vehicle in which to keep a car seat. Tanner asked Maria if he could use the truck. She said yes and had hired both he and Doc on as security.

"I'm not a security guard," Doc had complained privately. When Tanner pointed out that it paid better and was easier work than mucking out stalls, Doc agreed to take the job.

They would be off the books and paid in cash. Maria

also told them they would take it a day at a time, but that Tanner was off to a good start by ridding her of the Harvey brothers, who had been a nuisance for days.

There was no Mr. Reyes, other than Maria's teenage son, Javier. Her husband, Diego Reyes, had died a year earlier from a heart attack. However, Maria did have her children. Along with nineteen-year-old Javier, there was a sixteen-year-old daughter named Romina.

As far as Tanner could tell, he and Doc were the only employees who would be living on-site, other than a housekeeper and cook named Mrs. Salgado, who had her own room inside the home.

Mrs. Salgado was an energetic woman with long white hair. She had been with the family even before they moved to the United States from Mexico, the same year Maria gave birth to Romina.

Tanner met Mrs. Salgado as he and Doc entered the home for dinner at Maria's request. Tanner and Doc were escorted to the living room, where they were to wait until they were called to eat.

Doc settled in a recliner and turned on the flat screen TV that hung on the opposite wall.

"This is a real nice place, and even bigger than the old Parker house."

"You knew Frank Parker?"

"I used to play poker with him, and McKay too, but that was a long time ago. I even delivered Parker's kids right in this house. Well, I mean the old house."

Tanner walked over and stared down at Doc. "You're Dr. Richards, Graham Richards?"

"Yeah, but how do you know that?"

"I heard the name mentioned years ago."

Doc stared up at him. "Do I know you? I mean back in

the old days, but no, you'd be too young. I crawled into a bottle when you were just a kid."

"Do you still drink?"

Doc reached into his pocket and pulled out a bronze medallion, which Tanner recognized as being a sobriety chip.

"I haven't taken a drink in over five and a half years. And I'll tell you something, I hope this job works out. I need to settle down somewhere. I'm too old to keep living hand-to-mouth."

Footsteps came from the hall. When Tanner looked that way, he saw a girl standing in the doorway. It was Maria's daughter, Romina. When the beautiful sixteen-year-old spotted Tanner, her eyes widened, and she smiled.

"Hi."

"Hello. Are you Romina?"

She nodded, and Tanner thought she looked like a younger version of her mother, with the same long lustrous hair, large eyes, and smooth light brown skin.

"Are you two the guards Mom hired?"

"Yes."

Romina looked at Doc and made a face. "He looks too old to guard someone."

"Right now, he's guarding the TV remote."

Romina laughed and pointed down the hallway. "I have to go help Mrs. Salgado."

"We'll see you later," Tanner said, and Romina sent him a wave and walked toward the kitchen.

Doc smiled. "She thinks I'm an old geezer, but she sure took a shine to you."

"You are an old geezer, and she's just a kid," Tanner said.

Romina seemed well behaved to Tanner, but her brother impressed him as being a punk, as he sat across from Javier at the dinner table inside the Reyes' home.

The tattooed, muscular, and smug-looking Javier said very little, but he eyed Tanner as if he were an intruder, rather than a guard. From what Tanner gathered, Maria's son neither worked on the ranch nor went to school, meaning that the boy had no sense of responsibility.

And although he didn't say much, Javier did have questions for Tanner.

"What's your experience?"

"I recently disarmed and ran off the two men blocking your driveway, if that's any help."

"How do we know you're not really working for Chuck Willis?"

"I guess you don't and I'll have to prove myself."

"Yeah, you will," Javier said, and then he stayed silent and sulky during the rest of the meal.

Although, Tanner did notice that Javier bristled whenever Romina spoke to him. He wondered if the boy thought he had eyes for his sister. If that's what Javier was thinking, the kid could relax. Romina was a beauty, but too young. Tanner spent more time admiring her mother, Maria, even if the woman was ten years his senior.

However, Doc was right about Romina taking a liking to Tanner. The teenager sat beside him and hung on every word he said.

But, Maria did most of the talking, as she explained that Chuck Willis, a land developer and businessman, had made several offers for a section of her property. After she turned him down repeatedly, the ranch and its workers began to suffer "accidents."

Willis denied his involvement, but Maria didn't believe the man.

"It also doesn't help that people think the land is cursed," Romina said.

When Tanner asked her what she meant by that, her eyes lit up. "Some people in town say that there are ghosts here, but we've never seen any."

"Whose ghosts would they be?" Tanner asked, and Maria sat her wine glass down and cleared her throat.

"This land has a sad history; it's the main reason that my husband and I got such a good deal when we bought it years ago."

Doc spoke up. "We both know that this used to be the Parker Ranch."

Maria looked relieved that she wouldn't have to explain. "Oh good. And no one has ever claimed to see a ghost here… only at the cemetery."

Romina turned in her seat to face Tanner. "Why don't we go for a walk after dinner and I'll show you the graves."

Doc looked perplexed. "A walk? The town cemetery is a long ways off."

"They're not buried there," Romina said. "They were buried on this land."

"All of them?" Doc said.

Romina nodded. "Mm-hmm, the entire Parker family, and they were all killed on the same night, even the poor baby."

Tanner pushed his plate aside, as his appetite had gone away.

~

THE FIRST THING TANNER NOTICED ABOUT THE GRAVES WAS that they had been cared for. The grass around them was trimmed and the picket fence surrounding the small graveyard had been recently whitewashed.

One of the graves was older than the others were. It contained the body of Frank Parker's first wife. He had been laid to rest beside her, while his second wife, Claire, was buried on his opposite side.

Maria and Doc had come along with Tanner and Romina, but stood outside the fence, as Romina walked near the graves with Tanner.

"Who's been keeping things so neat?"

Romina smiled. "I do. Ever since I wrote a report about the Parkers last year for history class. I don't know, it just felt right to take care of them."

"You wrote about what happened here?"

"Yeah, and I got an A too."

"Thank you for caring for the graves."

"Why are you thanking me?"

"Someone should."

They moved down the line of headstones until they reached the last one, which had the name Cody Parker engraved on it.

Tanner took several deep breaths and then sniffled. When Romina looked at him, she saw that his eyes had grown moist.

"Are you all right?"

Tanner nodded and gestured at the graves. "It's sad, that's all."

Romina touched him on the arm. "You're very sensitive, aren't you?"

"Not usually, no."

Maria called her daughter's name and Romina walked off to join her mother beyond the fence.

Tanner sat back on his haunches and looked down the line of graves.

"I failed you all and I'm so sorry."

One last look at Cody Parker's grave and Tanner left the cemetery with a new resolve. Whatever was going on at the Reyes Ranch, he would not let history repeat itself. Even if it cost him his life, he would protect this family.

No, he would not fail again.

8
HELL HATH NO FURY

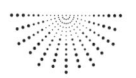

THE PARKER RANCH, SEPTEMBER 1997

Tanner smiled in admiration of Cody Parker's skill with a rifle.

The two of them were in a pasture and firing at a line of soda cans that were hanging from a tree limb. They had started the shooting contest at fifty yards, with the intention that the first one to miss had to pay to replace the soda. After blowing apart nearly two dozen cans, it didn't appear that either of them would miss.

They had an audience, as Cody's twin sisters and their friend, Tonya, watched the match. All three girls cheered Cody on.

The girls had been to school earlier, while Cody worked. Although only sixteen, he was already a high school graduate after having skipped two years. Cody worked full-time on the ranch. His father paid him a salary like any other hand, and Cody was banking it all with plans to someday travel and see the world.

Tanner backed up as far as he could and stood before a white wooden fence. There were four cans of soda left and they had moved hundreds of yards away and slightly downhill.

Tanner sighted on the next can in line, adjusted by feel for the wind and height, and then squeezed the trigger.

Nearly a quarter of a mile away, the soda can jerked on its string as its contents fizzed and splattered the grass below it.

Cody took the rifle from Tanner, looked through the scope, and blasted the last three remaining cans one after the other.

"Damn, Cody. If you're not a natural marksman then I don't know who is," Tanner said.

Tonya smiled and clapped for Cody. "He's the best!"

Cody smiled back at her and the little girl practically melted.

"Say now," Cody said to his sisters. "Don't you girls have chores to do?"

They answered him in stereo. "Yes."

"Then go on now. And don't make Tonya work, she's a guest here."

"I don't mind helping," Tonya said, and she sent Cody a little wave, as she followed his sisters, who were walking off toward the barn.

"All three of those girls are gonna break hearts someday," Tanner said. "And that Tonya already has her eye on you."

"She's just a baby."

"Yeah, now she is, but I bet you'll be eyeing her yourself in ten years."

"I won't be here in ten years. I want to travel a bit before I come back here to stay."

"You could join the army or the navy for that."

Cody shook his head. "I wouldn't last a day. I'm not big on taking orders from anyone."

"I hear you, but if you did join, they'd place you in a sniper program, because I swear, Cody, I've never seen anyone shoot better."

Cody grinned at Tanner. "You're damn good yourself; McKay's men won't stand a chance."

Tanner looked at Cody with a serious expression. "I meant what I said yesterday. Killing a man is not like killing an animal or hitting a target. Also, if you hesitate, you're liable to wind up dead."

"I hear what you're saying. I guess I'll find out what I'm made of when the time comes."

"That time won't come for you, not as long as I'm here. If McKay sends someone, I'll kill them."

Cody leaned back against the fence. "Is that really how you make your living, by killing?"

"It is."

"Were you ever a military sniper?"

"No, like you, I'm not big on following orders. It's why I'm my own boss."

"As a gun for hire?"

"More or less."

"It sounds better than most work, but… if it was me, I wouldn't kill just anybody, I'd want to know they had it coming."

"We all got it coming, Cody. God will see to that. No matter who you are or what you do, you'll die. I figure that when I kill someone, I really haven't changed anything, just sped things up."

"I get that. It's like when my mother died. I was sad, and I missed her, I still miss her, but it made me understand that death was real, and we don't get second chances."

Tanner fed fresh shells into the rifle as he spoke. "I take it you don't believe in an afterlife then?"

Cody shrugged. "I don't know if life goes on or not, but I know this, it won't be this life. And whatever happens after you die, it won't be happening to me. If I died and woke up somewhere else, I'd be as different to the me I am now, as I am to the baby I once was, you know? And heaven? I mean, what the hell is that? Wouldn't heaven have to be different for everyone, or else it wouldn't be heaven, it would just be another place, only cleaner maybe."

Tanner laughed. "You're a deep thinker, but I have to say, I see things pretty much the same way."

A voice called out from behind them and they turned to see Claire waving them in, as she held the baby in her other arm.

"Looks like your stepmom wants you."

Cody acknowledged Claire with a wave of his own. "Maybe she wants to go to the market. She doesn't drive, do you believe that?"

"She must be a city girl," Tanner said.

"She is."

"About that shopping."

"Yeah?"

Tanner tossed a thumb back at the tree, where some of the cans were still dripping. "Don't forget to buy more soda."

Cody laughed, then he and Tanner hopped over the fence and headed back toward the house.

∽

At the McKay Ranch, Jack Sheer hobbled into his boss's office on a pair of crutches, while his left foot wore a cast.

McKay sent his foreman a look of disgust. "Not only did Tanner almost kill you, but he stole your work truck too. Would you like to know where it was found?"

"You found my truck, where is it?"

"It was left outside the Parker Ranch with the keys in it."

Sheer looked down at his cast. "I can't even drive it, it's got a clutch, so I've been using my car to get around."

"Did you hear what I said? It was at the Parker Ranch, which means that Tanner told Parker my plans."

Sheer shrugged. "Those plans are no big secret. You wanted to hire Tanner to kill Parker, am I right?"

Sheer had settled on a red leather sofa on the left side of the room. McKay walked over with a drink in his hand and stared down at him with feverish eyes.

"I want Frank Parker dead. Hell yes, I do, and I could have paid you to do that. I also want that whore Claire dead as well, and before either of them gets it, I want Parker to see his children die. That's what I asked Tanner to do for me, and yeah, I'd like to keep it a secret."

Sheer looked away from his boss, whose bloodshot eyes bordered on madness.

McKay stared down at him for several seconds, but then walked over and plopped into the chair behind his desk, which caused the ice cubes inside his glass to clink loudly.

When Sheer spoke again, McKay almost didn't hear it. "What was that?"

"I said I'm not up to that, not killing kids, but I know a guy, not here, down in Mexico. He's part of a drug gang. Him and his people… they'll do anything."

McKay sat up straight in his chair, as his eyes brightened with interest. "Can you get in contact with this guy?"

"I think so, but I'll have to go to Mexico."

"Then go. But how much do you think he'll want?"

"His men will kill anybody he tells them to, even Claire's baby, but it won't be cheap."

"What's your guess?"

Sheer named a figure and McKay made a derisive sound. "Hell, Tanner would have cost me a lot more than that. I'll tell you what, Jack, I'll give you the amount you named plus five grand more, and whatever is left, you can keep, sort of as a fee for setting things up."

Sheer smiled wide. "You got a deal, Andy. I'll head to Mexico tomorrow."

"This stays between you and me, and when this shit goes down, I'll make sure we both have an alibi."

Sheer chuckled.

"What's so funny?"

"I was thinking about that old expression, you know the one, about hell having no fury like a woman scorned."

"Hell's got nothing on me either. When Claire left me for Parker and was fucking him behind my back, I became a laughingstock. But I'll get the last laugh and I'll see that whore dead."

Sheer grabbed his crutches and stood. "I'll leave for Mexico right after breakfast tomorrow."

McKay poured himself another drink. "You do that, Parker and that bitch can't die soon enough."

Sheer had reached the door when McKay called to him.

"Yeah, Andy?"

"This Mexican, tell him to take pictures and to make

sure that Claire knows I'm the one who sent him to kill her."

Sheer felt the hairs on the back of his neck stand up; he answered his boss with a shaky smile. "I'll do that," Sheer said, and then he hobbled on out of the office.

9

KILLING IS SO MUCH EASIER

Romina turned out to be a runner and a member of the high school track team. Although there were no meets scheduled, Romina trained year-round.

Tanner ran with her, while a nervous Doc stayed back at the ranch with the shotgun. Tanner wasn't crazy about leaving Doc to guard the place alone, but he thought it was less of a risk than leaving Romina unguarded, and unlike the old days, he could be reached by phone at any time.

They had jogged to the high school track together. Tanner was happy to sit in the bleachers and watch the swift girl complete her training laps, among a few other early morning runners who were mostly kids. He was still weakened from the shooting, and his ribs hurt when he ran, so the rest felt good.

The new high school had been built three years earlier, as the town began expanding. It looked nothing like the old one, which had been a beige brick building that resembled a prison. The whole town had changed drastically over the years, and as far as Tanner could see, the changes had all been for the better.

One of the other runners, a woman, was staring at him from where she stood and stretched, near the fence that circled the track. As Romina ran by, the woman pointed at Tanner and said something to Romina, who nodded to the woman and kept running.

The auburn-haired woman headed toward Tanner. As she came up the steps, Tanner could see that she was in her late twenties and very attractive, with large blue eyes that seemed to sparkle in the newly risen sun.

Tanner gestured at Romina. "You asked her if she knew me, didn't you?"

The woman smiled, and before answering, her eyes studied Tanner. "I was just making sure you weren't a pervert checking out the high school girls. It happens more often than you'd think. By the way, my name is Tonya Jennings."

Tonya extended her hand as she said her name, and she noticed that Tanner hesitated before shaking it. She then studied him closer, as something about him seemed familiar.

"Have we met before, Mr....?"

"Tanner, just call me Tanner. And yes, we may have met at some point, but I haven't been in this area for nearly twenty years."

"I was just a girl back then."

"And what are you now?" Tanner said, while still holding her hand.

Tonya's cheeks reddened slightly, and she gave a little laugh. "I'm all woman now, Tanner, and I think there might be a little pervert in you after all."

"Guilty," Tanner said, then he asked Tonya a question as she sat beside him. She was wearing a jogging outfit, which consisted of a long-sleeve white T-shirt and a flattering pair of black Spandex pants. "Are you a teacher too?"

"I am a teacher, but why did you ask it like that?"

"What do you mean?"

"It's just that, my mother is also a teacher, retired now. Usually, people know about her when they ask if I'm a teacher too, like you did, instead of simply asking if I were a teacher."

"Let me guess, you teach grammar?"

Tonya laughed. "I actually teach math. Now tell me something, how do you know Romina?"

Tanner explained that he had been hired on as security. When he gave the reason why, Tonya shook her head.

"I'm sorry, I know about the problems at the ranch, but I also know Chuck Willis and I find it hard to believe that he would be using such tactics. Mr. Willis is a good man who has done a lot for this town."

"Do you know him well?"

"I do. I'm dating his executive assistant, Trey Broderick."

"Lucky Trey, and as far as Willis goes, Maria Reyes is convinced that he wants her land."

"I don't know about the land, but Mr. Willis is not the ruthless type."

Romina finished her training and bounded up the stairs, looking sweaty, but barely breathing hard after running five miles.

She kissed Tonya on the cheek and smiled at Tanner. "Ms. Jennings is my favorite teacher. She also tutors me for free."

"Not for free," Tonya said, as she stood. "I do it so I can enjoy Mrs. Salgado's cooking, and I'll be by tonight to help you study for your test."

Tanner stood. "I guess I'll see you later."

Tonya nodded absently as she studied Tanner again. "I'm sure we've met before. What's your first name, Tanner?"

"It's just Tanner."

Tonya smiled. "Just Tanner? No, I would have remembered a man with only one name. I guess you remind me of someone, it's something about your eyes."

"Have a good day, Tonya."

"You too, Tanner."

Romina watched Tanner, as he watched Tonya Jennings walk down the bleacher steps and head toward the track.

"She's got a boyfriend."

"So she said."

"You like her?"

"What's not to like?"

"She's a great teacher; she can even make math fun."

Tanner took out his phone and checked the time. "We should get back."

They jogged toward the ranch along the shoulder of the road, but walked the second half so that Romina could cool down after her run.

"Would you date me if I was a little older, Tanner?"

"I might, but you're not older."

"I know. I just wondered if you liked me."

"I like you fine, but you must have a boyfriend."

"I do, but he's changed. I think I'm going to break up with him today."

"How has he changed?"

Romina gave a little shrug. "I've smoked pot, you know, but Billy, that's my boyfriend, he's really gotten into drugs, like coke. I think he's even tried heroin. That's not for me. I guess we're just going in different directions."

"Don't worry; you'll have no problem finding volunteers to replace him."

She smiled shyly. "I've already become friends with a boy at school and he's told me that he likes me a lot."

"Good."

"Not good."

"Why not?"

Romina stopped walking. "His dad is Chuck Willis."

Tanner looked at her. "Just how much do you like this Willis boy?"

"A lot, but I don't know if I should date him, you know, with what's going on with our parents and all."

Tanner sighed. Guarding people was much more complicated than just killing them.

"I think I'll go talk to Willis and find out what he wants."

Romina kissed him on the cheek. "Thank you, Tanner. I'll put in a good word for you with Miss Jennings. I don't like her boyfriend."

"Why don't you like him?"

"He's too pretty, and he's always working. She'd be much better off with you."

"I won't be here very long though, just long enough to find out what's going on."

"You don't think that Mr. Willis is behind everything?"

"I don't know; it's why I want to meet him."

They continued walking back toward the ranch. As they stepped around the final curve in the road, Tanner saw that they had visitors.

The Harvey brothers were back.

10

FRIENDS WITH BENEFITS

THE PARKER RANCH, SEPTEMBER 1997

Claire had waved Cody in, not to go shopping, but because he had a visitor. Cody's visitor was so beautiful that Tanner envied the boy. The girl's name was Raven, and it fit the dark-haired, dark-eyed beauty well.

Cody introduced Raven to Tanner, then the two of them headed upstairs to his room, as Claire watched them with disapproval registering on her face.

"What's the matter, Mrs. Parker, you don't like Cody's girlfriend?" Tanner asked.

Claire turned and stared at him. "That's not his girlfriend. She's Jimmy Kyle's girl, the kid that quarterbacks the football team."

Tanner grinned. "So, ah, she and Cody are just friends, is that it?"

"No, that is not it. She sneaks over here to see him just for sex. I also had to end a friendship with someone I caught coming out of his room when I arrived back home unexpectedly, a grown woman in her thirties."

Tanner's grin widened as he ran a hand over his beard. "The kid's got game."

"You find Cody's sexual escapades amusing, Mr. Tanner?"

"A little, but mostly I envy him. Raven is very beautiful."

The look of disapproval was back in Claire's eyes, but this time it was aimed at Tanner.

"Men. All you care about is sex."

Tanner looked at the baby in Claire's arms. Baby James, who was conceived while she was married to McKay and sleeping with Frank Parker behind McKay's back.

"Well now, Mrs. Parker, we can't all be as pure as you."

Claire caught his meaning and her cheeks reddened.

"Shouldn't you be doing something? Or is my husband paying you to stand around and talk?"

"Your husband is paying me to keep you safe, because your ex-husband has gone off the rails."

Claire bit her lower lip and then tossed her head to the right. "Follow me to the kitchen, Mr. Tanner. I want to hear about this meeting you had with Andy."

"I could go for a cup of java, and the name is just Tanner."

∽

THEY HAD COFFEE AT THE KITCHEN TABLE WHILE THE BABY sat in his high chair and gummed animal crackers. Tanner relayed to Claire the story he had told her husband, Frank Parker, only he left out the part about McKay wanting the children dead.

When he was done speaking, he saw Claire shudder. Her hand shook as she lowered her mug of coffee onto the kitchen table.

"He must be mad. I cheated on him, but I never rubbed it in. Once I realized I had fallen in love with Frank I asked Andy for a divorce."

"What was his reaction at the time?"

Claire pointed at her face. "He hit me. It closed my left eye and rendered me unconscious. I woke up in the hospital, and when I was discharged, I came here to live."

"Parker should have killed McKay right then and there for laying a hand on you."

Claire cocked her head and stared at him. "Cody said the very same words at the time. You and my stepson are much alike. You think that violence is a cure-all for every problem."

"It does solve many problems, but not all. And you never know when you'll need a gun."

"That's ridiculous. No one *needs* a gun. If you ask me, there are too many people carrying them in this state."

"Where are you from, Claire?"

"New York City, but I left there years ago."

"Maybe, but it hasn't left you."

That made Claire smile. "Where are you from, Tanner?"

"Here and there. My old man was a farm equipment salesman who never stayed in the same town for more than a year. Luckily for me, I like to travel."

"Have you been a bodyguard for long?"

"Bodyguard?"

"That's what you do, isn't it?"

Tanner knew the truth would frighten her and only complicate matters. He himself wasn't sure why he was guarding this family, other than the affinity he felt with Cody Parker.

"Yeah," Tanner said. "That's what I do. I keep people safe."

And as if it were a reaction to his blatant lie, baby James threw up.

11

ROUND TWO

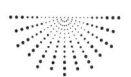

The Harvey brothers, Ernie and Rich, stepped from their pickup truck as Tanner and Romina approached the entrance of the Reyes Ranch.

Both men were bigger than Tanner and each one outweighed him by thirty pounds. As they walked toward him, they stood with straight backs and their arms held out slightly from their sides, in a subconscious effort to appear as huge as they could.

Tanner told Romina to head to the barn and find Doc, so that the older man could return with the shotgun. Curiosity overcame the girl, and after walking just a few steps down the driveway, she turned to see what would happen next.

If the brothers had acquired new weapons since Tanner took their guns away, they didn't display them. By the sneers lighting their faces, Tanner could tell they just wanted to kick his ass.

His gun was secured against the small of his back. He decided to leave it there unless needed. Ernie, the one with darker hair, came at him from the left, while Rich approached from the front. Tanner raised his hands up to shoulder height and took a step backwards, as he feigned being intimidated.

It worked. After sharing a smug, knowing look with each other, the brothers relaxed and sauntered toward Tanner, who still stood with his hands up, as if to say that he didn't want any trouble.

Had they been paying attention, the Harvey brothers might have noticed that the fingers of Tanner's hands were straight and pressed together with the thumbs tucked in, and they might have had a chance to block his first blows.

As the men crowded in on him, and Ernie was about to take hold of his shirt, Tanner jabbed his stiff fingers into the men's throats.

Ernie got the worst of it, as he was closer. He stumbled backwards while clutching his neck with both hands, as a raspy, guttural moan fell from his lips.

The blow hurt Rich, but after coughing once and moving away from Tanner, he was red-faced with fury and came charging in.

Tanner waited until Rich was almost upon him, then he dropped flat to the ground. Unable to halt his forward momentum, Rich tripped over Tanner and came down hard on his right knee.

He then spent the next thirty seconds hissing through his teeth in pain, as he rocked on the ground clutching his leg, with his bare knee showing. The knee was scraped and bloody beneath the torn fabric of his twill pants.

Tanner walked over and looked down at Ernie, who was lying on his back in the street and gasping for breath. His face was a bright pink and he gazed back at Tanner with frightened eyes.

"Can't… breathe."

Tanner called to Rich, who was just rising from the ground. "Your brother needs a doctor."

Concern lit Rich's face as he hobbled over with the bad knee to check out his brother.

"Oh shit, what did you do to him?"

"I taught him to never fuck with me again."

Rich glared at Tanner, then his gaze grew less harsh. "I need help. With this knee, I'll never get him in the truck by myself."

Tanner reached down and grabbed Ernie beneath the left arm. After Rich took his right, they dragged the wheezing, red-faced thug to the truck and piled him onto the passenger seat.

As Rich started the engine, Tanner removed the gun from his back and pointed it at Rich's face.

"Come at me again, or do anything to the Reyes family, and I will kill both of you."

Rich nodded as he stared at the gun, which Tanner had taken from him in their first encounter. After Tanner stepped back, Rich put the truck in gear, hung a U-turn, and sped off.

Romina ran to Tanner with a big grin showing and hugged him. "That was awesome!"

"Thanks for getting Doc."

"Oh, you didn't need him. You kicked both their asses."

"It would have been a different story if they knew what they were doing, but they're used to everyone being intimidated by their size."

"But you weren't, right?"

"No, I was. They're both bigger than I am. It's why I asked you to get Doc."

Romina looked abashed. "I should have gotten him, and I'm sorry, but I just couldn't not watch."

Tanner pointed toward the driveway entrance. "C'mon, you've got to get ready for school."

~

Once at the house and inside the kitchen, Romina recounted Tanner's fight with the Harvey brothers over breakfast. She did so in a very theatrical manner, which caused Maria and Doc to laugh, while Javier listened with an expression that said he found the tale to be a tall one.

"It sounds like you got lucky, Tanner," Javier said. "If either one of them had landed a punch on you the fight would have been over."

"That's why I made sure that they didn't," Tanner said.

After grunting, Javier grabbed a motorcycle helmet from the counter and went off to ride his bike, a Harley.

As everyone else rose from the table, Maria walked over and kissed Tanner on the cheek. "Thank you for protecting my daughter. I don't know what they would have done if she were alone."

"You're welcome, but we've spent enough time being on the defensive."

"What do you mean?"

"I want to talk to Chuck Willis, and I want you to come with me. Maybe we can keep things from escalating."

Maria's eyes grew fiery. "That man just sent thugs to my home. I may not be able to control my temper."

"I still think you should talk. Also, I want to get a feel for him."

Romina walked over and smiled up at Tanner. "Are you going to kick his ass too?"

Tanner looked at her and then at Maria.

"I'll do whatever it takes to keep you safe, count on it."

12

PABLO

STARK, TEXAS, SEPTEMBER 1997

At the McKay Ranch, three of the hands watched as Jack Sheer drove away, headed for Mexico.

The three men all went by nicknames. They were Slim, who was slim. Pug, who had a wrinkled face like a pug. And Okie, who was from Oklahoma. Okie was the biggest of the three and the other two followed him around.

Okie pointed at Sheer's departing truck. "Jack's going off to find someone who'll fix McKay's problem."

"What problem?" Slim said. "Having too much money?"

"I'm talking about that slut ex-wife of his. Everybody knows the man wants her dead."

Pug's wrinkles relaxed as he smiled. "I miss seeing that girl around here, she was fine as hell."

Okie spit tobacco juice into the dirt before he spoke. "She was a slut, sleeping around with Parker behind

McKay's back. I tell you boys, McKay will pay a pretty penny to see her dead."

Slim narrowed his eyes. "What are you saying, Okie, you want to kill her?"

"Think about it. Somebody is gonna whack her for McKay sooner or later. If we did it, no one would suspect. When we bring McKay proof that she's dead, he'll pay us, and I bet he pays us good."

Slim shook his head. "I know we beat them two fags to death that time we was drunk in Dallas, but I never killed a woman."

"Hell, I'll kill her," Pug said. "What we do is, we steal a van, wear masks, and grab her while she's out somewhere."

Okie smiled in agreement. "Once we have her, we can take her out to that old well we found and dump her body in there."

Okie looked at Slim. "Are you in? Either we all do this, or none of us, because one man has to drive and run interference while the other two grab her."

Slim nibbled at his lower lip, but then nodded. "Yeah, I'm in, but listen, before we kill her… I say we fuck her."

Both Okie and Pug looked at Slim as if he were stupid.

"Well, hell yes, we'll fuck her," Pug said. "Anything else would be a goddamn shame."

∽

AT THE PARKER RANCH, CODY WATCHED WITH GROWING curiosity as his eleven-year-old twin sisters walked toward the barn carrying food and a quart of milk.

He had just entered the kitchen when he caught sight of them through the window, their braided blonde ponytails bouncing along behind them as they rushed along, while still dressed in their pajamas, robes, and slippers.

Cody followed, but walked around to the side door, where he placed an ear to it. He heard the girls talking to someone. He entered the barn and realized that the girls were up in the loft.

Cody climbed the ladder as quietly as he could. When he raised his head up above floor level, and then continued up, the girls spun around, with Jill dropping the milk bottle, which thankfully didn't break after landing in straw.

There was a Mexican boy with them. He was a little older than Cody and wearing clothes that weren't much more than rags. He looked as if someone had recently given him a beating. Faded bruises covered his arms and face, while his left eye was puffy. Cody saw the boy swallow hard, and he also saw the fear in his eyes.

"What's going on here?"

Jill came over and took her brother's hand. "This is Pablo, Cody. We found him hiding in here a few days ago. And look, somebody beat him up."

"Why didn't you say something about him?"

"Tonya said we should, but we were afraid. We thought that Daddy or Claire might make him leave the ranch."

Cody walked closer and saw Pablo cringe as he if were expecting violence. "Hey, Pablo, my name is Cody. I won't hurt you."

"Neither will I," said a voice from behind. When Cody turned his head, he saw Tanner climbing up from the ladder.

Pablo said something in Spanish and Cody shook his head. "I speak a little Spanish, Pablo, but I don't know what you said."

"He said he didn't mean any harm and he'll leave," Tanner said, then he spoke to Pablo in Spanish, was answered, and after going back and forth several times, Tanner translated for Cody.

"He came across the border five days ago after both his parents drowned on their fishing boat. From what he says, it sounds like some of McKay's men gave him that beating after they caught him hiding in a tool shed."

Cody looked Pablo over and winced. "We'd better have a doctor look at him. He might have broken ribs, and I don't like the look of that eye."

"One more thing," Tanner said. "He's scared. He said that all he wants to do is go and… he begged not to be hurt again."

Little Jill wiped away a tear and took Pablo's hand. "Nobody will hurt you. Right, Cody?"

Cody smiled at Pablo, as he spoke to Tanner. "Tell him everything's cool and that he can stay."

Tanner relayed the message and Cody watched as Pablo visibly relaxed.

Jill and Jessie hugged their brother about the waist.

"He can really stay? What if Daddy wants him gone?" Jessie said.

"I'll handle Daddy, but once he's well, Pablo goes to work. We can use another hand anyway."

Cody sent the girls back to the house to get dressed. He and Tanner followed with Pablo, after the boy had eaten the food the girls had given him.

They were taking him to the house so he could get clean and change into some of Cody's clothes, as the boy was nearly his height.

Frank and Claire were entering the kitchen the same time that Tanner and Cody were bringing Pablo in through the back door. They stopped in their tracks and stared at them.

"Who's he?" Frank said, as he pointed at Pablo.

"His name is Pablo, Dad. He came across the border and had the bad luck of hiding out on McKay's ranch. Some of McKay's men beat him up like this."

Claire handed baby James to his father and went over to look at Pablo's wounds. When she spoke to him in Spanish and he answered, Cody raised an eyebrow in surprise.

"Where did you learn to speak Spanish?"

"In New York. My parents had a Spanish maid, and I grew up with her daughters. They were Puerto Rican, not Mexican, but we can understand each other."

She spoke to Pablo again and Cody saw Claire's gaze darken with sorrow.

"He's all alone, his parents are dead."

"Yeah, he told Tanner that. Tanner speaks Spanish too."

Claire looked back at her husband. "You must have something he can do on the ranch, no?"

Frank sighed. "He's a sorry-looking thing, but yeah, we'll keep him fed and he can sleep in the other guest room for now. But how bad off is he?"

Claire spoke to Pablo again.

"He says he's sore, but that nothing was broken, and he can see out of that swollen eye. He's probably right about being okay. If he had internal injuries, he wouldn't have an appetite."

Frank looked at his son. "He's all yours, Cody. See that he gets straightened out. We'll find a job for him around here after he heals up."

Pablo still looked apprehensive, but when Claire translated, he bowed his head repeatedly toward Frank while saying, "Gracias."

Frank smiled. "De nada, boy."

Cody led Pablo upstairs to get clean and Tanner settled at the table beside Frank, who was still holding the baby.

"It's good of you to take care of that boy," Tanner said.

Frank shrugged. "I only pray that someone would return the favor if one of my children were left all alone in this world."

"We'll never have to worry about that," Claire said, as she prepared the coffeemaker.

For some reason, her words sent a chill down Tanner's spine.

13

GUILTY OR INNOCENT?

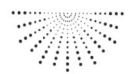

Willis Financial Services was located on the land that had once been the McKay Ranch. That made the trip there a short one for Tanner and Maria.

Tanner had gone shopping first and was wearing a new black suit without a tie, along with a pair of new boots. He also picked up the fake ID Tim Jackson sent him and confirmed that the farm back in Ridge Creek was being attended to by an acquaintance.

Tanner had to assume that Sara Blake had not only revealed that he was still alive, but also that he had been masquerading as Romeo all along. Once he settled things in Texas, he would have to head back to New York City and deal with the fallout. On the bright side, it would give him a chance to see Sophia Verona again, a thought that pleased him.

However, the downside was that he would also be walking back into a city where he was a marked man. Although, with the info he now had concerning the Conglomerate's financial dealings, he should have no trouble forging a truce.

He and Maria had arrived at Willis Financial without an appointment and Tanner expected to be kept waiting. He was surprised when they were ushered up to Willis's office almost right away.

The young security guard who escorted them was a large man in a spotless white shirt, black pants, and shoes that shined as if they were new.

The man was courteous and respectful toward them. Tanner began to think that Chuck Willis was either innocent of the campaign of harassment being waged against the Reyes Ranch, or too devious to make his intentions obvious.

The guard escorted them to the top floor of the six-story building, where they were handed off to Trey Broderick, who was Willis's executive assistant, and Tonya Jennings' boyfriend.

Trey was in his thirties, with golden hair coiffed in that way that only Ivy League School graduates seem to have perfected.

He was about Tanner's size, but there was a softness about him, along with the pallor he wore. Tanner wondered if the man ever went outside during daylight hours. Still, Trey Broderick was handsome. Tanner guessed it was his looks that drew Tonya to him.

Chuck Willis was in his mid-forties, divorced, and turned out to be nearly as handsome as his assistant. Willis was tall and slim. He greeted Maria with a smile that would have melted most female hearts; however, Maria answered it with a cold stare.

"Mrs. Reyes, it's good to see you again."

"Unfortunately, I cannot say the same, Mr. Willis. As a matter of fact, I think you know why."

"There's been more trouble at your ranch?"

"Yes. Two of your employees have been parked outside

the entrance to the ranch and intimidating anyone who attempted to seek employment with us. Or I should say almost anyone, as Mr. Tanner here drove them off twice."

"My employees? What are their names?"

"I'm speaking about the Harvey brothers. I was told by someone that they work on the loading dock here."

Willis's demeanor changed, and he snorted with disgust. "Those two men no longer work for me, not since one of my security personnel discovered they were selling drugs on company property, marijuana. That was nearly six months ago, and I assure you, Mrs. Reyes, I wish you and your ranch no harm."

Maria's gaze softened under Willis's seeming sincerity, but the next words out of Willis's mouth made her raise her guard again.

"By the way, I have a new offer concerning your land; do you have time to discuss it?"

Maria turned to Tanner with a look that said, "See what a sneaky weasel this man is?" She moved toward Willis until she was standing near enough to hug him, then looked up into his eyes.

"Listen to me, you bastard. I will never sell you that land. Send the Harvey brothers to harass us, send a damn army, and my answer will be the same. No! You will never have my land."

Willis appeared flustered, and as he opened his mouth to respond, Maria spun around and headed toward the door.

"We're leaving, Tanner."

"Please, wait," Willis said, but Maria kept going, and her heels clacked loudly against the tile floor as she headed toward the elevators.

Tanner gave Willis one last look and was puzzled by the appearance of what seemed to be sincere angst on the man's face. It was as if Maria's words not only wounded him, but that he dreaded her disapproval.

Trey Broderick's face displayed nothing, and Tanner wondered what part he played, if any, in what was happening at the ranch.

Tanner joined Maria by the elevators just as one opened. The last sight they saw before the doors closed was that of Willis, who walked over and gazed at Maria while once more proclaiming his innocence. His words were cut short by the closing of the doors.

"That man. Did you see how devious he was? First, he says he's as innocent as a lamb, but not two seconds passed before he was trying to get me to sell to him again. It makes me furious!"

They returned to the parking lot and climbed back in the truck. As Tanner signaled to turn right toward the ranch, Maria pointed left.

"Let's go into town. It's nearly lunch time and I need a drink."

"You're the boss," Tanner said, and drove toward the center of town.

14

CENTAVO-WISE AND PESO-FOOLISH

MATAMOROS, MEXICO, SEPTEMBER 1997

Jack Sheer hobbled along on his crutches into a bar on Avenida Marte R. Gómez and weaved his way toward the rear, where there were several young Mexican men wearing shoulder holsters. One of the men stopped him and asked him his business, while speaking English without an accent.

Sheer pointed to where four men sat in a booth with padded seats, which were covered in black-and-red leather squares. Three of the men weren't known to Sheer, but the fourth man, the man with his back to the wall and a clear view of the entrance was the man that Jack had come to see. The man greeted Sheer with a nod of recognition and signaled to the young man that it was acceptable to let him pass.

The man's name was Martillo, which was the Spanish word for hammer. It was a name he had carried since killing his first man with a claw hammer when he was only nine.

He was a thick-bodied man with huge hands. His squat head sat on his shoulders with no discernible neck visible above his collar. Martillo's dark shiny hair was worn down to his shoulders, and his eyebrows were like twin mustaches that had been placed over his dead eyes.

Martillo was an amateur chess player who liked to use the game's terminology whenever he discussed business, on the off chance that he was being recorded or overheard.

Martillo asked the other three men to leave the table, then he gestured for Sheer to take a seat.

Sheer wedged his ample gut into the booth and smiled. "Martillo, how are you?"

"I am good, Jack, and I've risen in stature since our last dealings."

Martillo's soft voice carried with it a strong accent, but he enunciated each English word carefully, so was easily understood.

"I'm glad, Martillo, because I have need of your expertise."

"I see, and how many pieces would you like to have removed from the board?"

"Six, and four of those are too young to play."

Martillo raised a bushy eyebrow. "That is unusual, and it will, of course, cost extra."

"We're prepared to pay."

"We?"

"I'm here for my boss."

"Ah, your king. And does your king know the rules of the game?"

"Yes," Sheer said.

The rules were that if any of Martillo's men were killed or injured, it would be up to McKay to make things right with a payment. If any of the men were captured, McKay had to see that they were given bail so they could flee back across the border. McKay and Sheer would also need to establish alibis for the time Martillo's men were performing their acts of slaughter.

"Are you certain, Jack? I will be sending four pawns to handle your problem, and I expect all four of them to return in good health, two of which will be my nephews. If anything unfortunate occurs, the penalty will be a harsh one."

Sheer tired of speaking in code and leaned across the table to whisper. "The man your men will be facing, he and his teenage son will be armed, but with nothing more than rifles. Those silenced room brooms your men carry will clean his clock before he knows it."

The "silenced room brooms" that Sheer spoke of were Heckler & Koch MP5 submachine guns with sound suppressors attached.

Martillo whispered back, although his face displayed annoyance that Jack broke protocol.

"I do not know this phrase concerning the clean clock, but yes, the 'brooms' you speak of are vastly superior to most other cleaning tools."

The talk turned to details and money, which were written on a pad of paper and passed back and forth until the deal was set. Afterwards, Martillo once again issued a warning.

"Remember, my pawns remain in good health or your king and I will have a problem. Are you certain that all they'll be facing is this other king and his young knight? If not, we must renegotiate, and I'll send more pawns."

Sheer thought of Tanner and his warning to leave the Parker family in peace, but he was certain the gun for hire had moved on and would not be a factor. And if Tanner was there, what could he do against four hardened killers with superior weapons?

Also, Martillo had charged more for his services than Sheer expected, and the more money Martillo was paid, the less there would be left as payment for setting things up.

Sheer smiled. "There won't be any problems."

In the days ahead, he would have cause to regret uttering those words.

15

RISKY BUSINESS

Maria and Tanner had ordered lunch along with their drinks inside a restaurant that Tanner remembered from the old days, although the decor and menu had improved over the years.

Maria took a sip of her second drink, then smiled at Tanner. "My daughter has a crush on you."

"She might, but she also has her eyes on someone else at her school."

Maria sat her drink down. "Please tell me that means she's breaking up with that boyfriend of hers."

"It does. I take it you don't like him?"

"Billy was a good boy, but that's changed. I had to send him away last week when he came to the house to pick up Romina. I smelled liquor on his breath. He wasn't drunk mind you, but he wasn't driving my daughter anywhere intoxicated. Romina and I argued about it, but I guess she's come to realize that she can do better."

"The boy she's interested in now is Willis' son."

"No."

"Yes."

"Damn."

They finished their meal and Tanner leaned back and watched Maria.

"I have a theory about Willis," he said.

"And what's that?"

"I think the man wants you, not your land."

Maria had been taking a sip of her drink as Tanner spoke. She nearly spat it out in surprise.

"You think Chuck Willis wants to be with me?"

"Yes, and I also believed him when he said he knew nothing about what the Harvey brothers were up to. If that's true and he's innocent, then there's someone else pulling the strings. Who else besides Willis would want your land?"

"No one; or at least no one else has shown interest."

"It's just a theory, but I'm good at reading people and Willis doesn't strike me as devious."

Maria held up a finger. "Or, he's very good at fooling people, even you."

"That's a possibility," Tanner admitted.

Maria finished her drink and refused a third, and soon they were back on the road.

"What about you, Tanner, is there anyone in your life?"

"No, I guess you'd say I'm a loner."

"Have you always been like that?"

"Yes."

"You're afraid of commitment?"

"I don't trust the emotion of love, not romantic love."

"Love doesn't always end badly."

"Maybe not, but why take the chance?"

Maria laughed. "What else in life is worth the risk?"

Tanner thought about that and found he didn't have an answer.

16

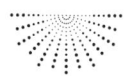

RED SAUCE

STARK, TEXAS, SEPTEMBER 1997

Okie, Pug, and Slim made their move on Claire in the supermarket parking lot.

While Cody was securing the food into the bed of the pickup truck, Claire was fastening the baby into his car seat. Cody had just enough time to see the masked figures of Pug and Slim grab Claire, before sensing Okie rushing up on him from the rear.

Okie had been aiming his blackjack at a spot behind Cody's right ear, but the boy moved at the last second and the sap only caught him a glancing blow on the shoulder.

Okie raised the blackjack high in preparation to deliver another blow and Cody smashed a large jar of spaghetti sauce against his forehead.

Okie cried out in agony, as shards of glass penetrated the stocking he wore over his head and a sliver entered his left eye. In the meantime, Cody had looked back to see Claire struggling to get free.

Pug kept one hand clamped over Claire's mouth, as he lifted her and prepared to toss her into the back of the van they'd stolen. Slim followed along, as he tried to keep his hold on Claire's kicking legs.

Cody fought the urge to run toward them and fight. Instead, he headed for the cab of the pickup, where his rifle was secured in its rack.

Pug noticed him first. As Cody sighted over the roof of the truck, he cried out a warning to Slim. "The boy's got a rifle!"

Both men dropped Claire unceremoniously to the parking lot pavement as they reached for the guns stuck in their belts. Pug kept his weapon secured behind his back. He barely managed to clear it before Cody's first shot removed the top of his head and sent it landing inside the van. Slim did a bit better. He was an instant away from pulling the trigger when Cody sent two into his chest and shredded his lungs and heart.

A shot pinged off the door frame and ricocheted into the pickup's windshield, shattering it. It was Okie, with the stocking removed. He was firing at Cody with his one good eye, which was set in a face covered with spaghetti sauce and blood. The two liquids were distinguishable only by their texture, as the color of the fluids matched.

Cody swung the rifle around and fired a shot that entered Okie's remaining eye. It sent the big man crumbling to the ground with the back of his head blown away.

"My baby!" Claire shouted. She scrambled to her feet, while her shoes slipped amid the blood of her would-be captors. Baby James was wailing in the aftermath of the chaos, but he had been uninjured by gunfire, or the shattered glass of the windshield.

Cody walked over and kicked the gun from Okie's hand, despite knowing that his shot must have killed the man. Slim and Pug had dropped their weapons as they fell. Cody let them be and walked back over to Claire, who was trying to calm the baby cradled in her arms.

Claire had scraped her left elbow after being dropped. The wound was bleeding, but she seemed not to notice. She gazed about and took in the scenes of death surrounding her, while the other shoppers in the parking lot began converging to gawk.

"Are you all right, Claire?" Cody asked, as he laid his rifle on the truck's front seat.

"You... you killed them?"

"Yes."

"Oh my God!"

"It was them or us. How is James doing?"

"He'll be all right, but I want to go home."

Cody pointed toward the street, where a police car was rushing toward the supermarket entrance.

"I think we have to deal with him first."

Seconds later, the police car skidded to a stop near the truck and County Sheriff Emory McKay stepped out with a gun in his hand. He was Andy McKay's older brother and resembled him, but the sheriff was shorter and had gray hair. He was also Claire's former brother-in-law. The first words out of his mouth were directed at her.

"What kind of shit have you caused now, Claire?"

Cody raised his empty hands in the air where everyone could see them. He spoke to the people in the crowd. "You people see that I'm unarmed, right?"

The sheriff walked over and got in Cody's face. "What are you trying to say, boy? You think that I would shoot you without cause?"

"If you're anything like your brother you would."

Three seconds later, Cody was slammed onto the hood of his truck and having his hands cuffed behind his back.

17

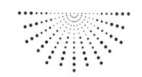

PUNK ASS

Javier rushed toward the truck with Doc following behind him, as Maria and Tanner arrived back at the ranch house.

"I tried calling you, Mom. Where were you for so long?"

Maria checked her phone and saw that she had forgotten to turn it on. "Oh sorry, I had it turned off. Tanner and I stopped for lunch."

"And drinks," Javier said, after catching the scent of alcohol on his mother's breath. He walked over to stand in front of Tanner. "What are you up to? Are you trying to get in my mother's pants?"

"I'm not her type, but that would be up to her, wouldn't it?"

Despite being still in his teens, Javier was taller than Tanner, and bigger. Those two facts gave Javier courage, despite knowing that Tanner had recently defeated two men who were each even larger than he was.

"I want you to stay away from my sister too. She doesn't need a babysitter when she runs."

Maria clapped her hands together to grab Javier's attention, but the young man just kept staring into Tanner's eyes in an attempt to intimidate him.

"Javier, leave Mr. Tanner alone. You should be thanking him for guarding Romina this morning. If he hadn't been there, who knows what the Harvey brothers might have done."

Javier broke eye contact and shrugged. "Maybe you're right, Mom." Javier turned away from Tanner, but then spun back to deliver a punch to Tanner's face.

Tanner had seen it coming, ducked the punch, and backhanded Javier with a swat at his nose, which caused it to bleed.

Javier scurried backwards in shock, touched his face, then stared in surprise at the blood on his fingers. "You broke my fucking nose!"

Doc came over and told Javier to tilt his head back. When he touched Javier's nose, the boy let out a cry of pain.

"It's not broken, but it is likely to swell up. Maybe that will teach you not to throw a sucker punch. Not everyone is a sucker."

Javier pushed Doc away. "Fuck you, old man."

"Javier!" Maria cried, but the boy kept walking toward the house.

When she turned to look at Tanner, she sent him a sad smile. "Thank you for not hurting him worse, and he needed to be taught a lesson. He's been getting out of hand since his father passed away."

"He's still young," Tanner said, and let it go at that. What point would there be in telling the woman that her only son was a punk?

THE LIFE & DEATH OF CODY PARKER

TANNER PICKED UP ROMINA FROM SCHOOL WITHOUT incident. Later that afternoon, he was pleased when Tonya Jennings showed up at the ranch to tutor Romina.

Tanner had been seated on the porch with Doc, teaching the old man how to clean a gun. When Tonya arrived, Tanner introduced her to Doc. She joined them around the folding card table they were using.

"I haven't been shooting in months," Tonya said. "And I'm better with a rifle than a handgun."

Doc pointed at the rifle leaning on the wall near Tanner. It was an old Winchester Model 70, which had belonged to Maria's late husband. Tanner had cleaned it earlier, after buying fresh ammo for it.

"You should see this dude shoot. I lined up a bunch of tin cans on a fence post earlier and damn if he didn't hit every one of them."

Tonya smiled, but then grew pensive. "I used to visit this ranch often when the Parkers owned it, and Cody Parker was the best with a rifle I ever saw. But then there was that one time when the Parkers had a man staying here, and he tied Cody when they were shooting soda—" Tonya stopped talking in mid-sentence and stared at Tanner. "Have you ever been to the Reyes Ranch before, Tanner?"

"No, this is my first time."

Tonya cocked her head slightly as she studied his face. "Did you have a beard when you were younger?"

"No."

"And did you ever meet Cody Parker?"

"No," Tanner said, "I never met the boy."

Romina appeared, walked over, and kissed Tonya on the cheek. "Hi, Miss Jennings. Are you and Tanner getting to know each other better?"

Tonya nodded. "Yes, I think I do know him better than

I thought. As for you, young lady, it's time to study."

"Can't we talk with Tanner for a little while first?"

"Don't procrastinate, and say goodbye to Doc and Tanner."

Romina said goodbye reluctantly, and she and Tonya entered the house.

Doc turned in his seat and watched them go. "My teachers sure weren't that pretty, and I think she's got her eye on you."

"She already has a boyfriend."

"Have you ever let that stop you?"

"No."

Doc laughed. "I like you, boy. How's that wound coming along?"

"It's healing and my ribs barely hurt."

Doc looked around and sighed. "I like it here. I asked Maria if there was a chance I could stay on after the trouble passed."

"What did she say?"

"She said she'd think about it, but I wouldn't blame her if she said no. She probably figures my old ass isn't good for much and will hire a younger man."

The screen door opened and slammed shut, and Javier stood staring at them.

Doc called to him in a friendly voice. "How's it going there, Javier?"

Javier gave him the finger and sent a second one Tanner's way, before heading down the steps and straddling his motorcycle. It was an old Harley Davidson Road King that had seen better days.

"Being young doesn't give a man worth," Tanner said, and Doc flipped Javier the bird back as the boy rode off.

∽

Romina made certain that Tanner and Tonya were seated beside each other during dinner, and Tanner noticed the teacher giving him sideways glances throughout the meal.

Maria made a point of thanking Doc for fixing several things around the property, such as leaky faucets and a cracked windowpane. Tanner thought it bode well for the old man and his desire to stay on the ranch.

After dinner, Tanner walked Tonya out to her car, a ruby red Ford Fusion. The teacher asked him a question.

"Have you ever been married, Tanner?"

"There's no Mrs. Tanner, no, and by the way, I met Trey Broderick."

"You've met Trey? What did you think of him?"

"Not much."

Tonya fought back a smile. "Are you always so honest?"

"I find it keeps things simple."

Tonya stared into his eyes. "Oh, I think you are anything but simple. You're more like a mystery or a puzzle."

"Do you like puzzles?"

She moved closer. "I adore them."

"Why don't we go have a drink somewhere?" Tanner said.

Tonya took a step back and shook her head. "I can't. Trey is coming by and I have to get home."

"I see."

She opened her car door, gave him a look as if she were going to ask a question, but smiled instead.

"You have a good evening, Tanner."

"You too."

And as he watched Tonya drive away, Tanner wondered if she remembered him.

18

HERO

THE PARKER RANCH, SEPTEMBER 1997

Tanner was certain that if Sheriff Emory McKay wasn't wearing a badge, Frank Parker would have kicked the man's ass clear down to the Gulf of Mexico.

Three employees from the ranch owned by the sheriff's brother attacked Parker's wife and son, and McKay had the nerve to handcuff Cody for defending himself and keeping his stepmother safe, not to mention the baby, who also could have come to harm.

"My brother said he knows nothing about this attack. He also said that he doesn't hold a grudge against Claire, or you either, Frank."

"Your brother is lying," Tanner said.

The sheriff narrowed his eyes, as he looked Tanner's way. There was just the four of them in the living room: Frank Parker, Cody, the sheriff, and Tanner. Cody sat in a chair biting his tongue, as his father had told him to remain quiet.

"Let me see some ID, Tanner."

Tanner handed over his driver's license and the sheriff made a face. "This says your name is Tucker Coe, so why do you call yourself Tanner?"

"I don't know. Your name is Emory McKay, so why do you call yourself sheriff?"

"Are you getting smart with me, boy?"

"No, but I can tell you for a fact that your brother wants Claire Parker dead, because he tried to hire me to kill her."

The sheriff tossed the license back at Tanner. "The hell you say!"

"It's a fact. And since you're his brother, I'm betting you already know what a sick bastard he is."

The sheriff made a move toward Tanner, but then stopped himself and took several deep breaths.

When he was under control again, the sheriff held up a finger.

"All right. My brother does harbor bad feelings toward Claire, and who can blame him? But as near as I can tell, those three men acted alone. Now, I will go as far to say that they may have thought their actions would please my brother, but he did not order them to attack Claire."

"Think what you want, Emory, but what about my son?" Frank said.

"The boy is in the clear. The evidence and several witnesses back up his story."

Tanner smiled at Cody. "The boy, excuse me, the man is a hero."

The sheriff glared at Cody. "The boy has a smart mouth."

After the sheriff left, Frank headed upstairs to see to Claire and his other children. He stopped halfway up the stairs and looked back at Cody.

"Son?"

"Yeah, Dad?"

"Thank you, boy. I'd have died if anything happened to Claire."

Cody smiled. "She's beginning to grow on me too."

Frank laughed and then continued up.

Tanner walked over to Cody and stared down at him. "You did what had to be done, but how do you feel about it?"

"Killing those three men didn't bother me. They were trying to hurt Claire, and stepmother or not, she's a Parker. Nobody messes with my family and gets away with it."

Tanner tapped the gun he was wearing on his hip. "I think I'll keep this close, just in case."

"You don't think McKay is done, do you?"

"No."

"I don't know," Cody said. "Maybe after what happened today, he'll back off."

And even to his young ears, the words sounded like false hope.

∼

At the McKay Ranch, Jack Sheer was getting ready to tell McKay about his meeting with Martillo in Mexico, after having learned about Okie, Slim, and Pug's misadventure.

"The boy?" Sheer asked.

"The boy," McKay answered. "Cody, the kid killed all three of them and Emory says the boy was as cool as ice about it."

"I don't know what Slim, Pug, and Okie were thinking, but because of them, Parker will be on the alert. You're sure that Tanner is staying there too?"

"He is. These men you hired, are they going to be enough?"

Sheer smiled, as he tried to look more confident than he felt. "Tanner might be a pro, but he'll be going up against four men just like himself. And as far as the kid, Cody, he just got lucky today."

"You best be right. When it goes down you and I will be away from here, and we'll make sure we have people who can verify we weren't anywhere near the trouble."

"People will still suspect that you had it done."

"Let them, my damn brother included, but I can't go much longer without paying that bitch back."

"People around here will be talking about what happens to the Parkers for years."

McKay smiled. "The Parkers should all thank me; I'm about to make them famous."

The two men laughed, but if they knew how it all would end, they'd have cried.

19

SORRY HURTS TOO MUCH

Tanner walked out to the road to look around, but as he came back, he saw movement on the porch. It was 1:13 a.m., Maria and her brood should all be sound asleep.

He had taken to getting four hours of sleep after dinner and then keeping watch all night, in the belief that if anything happened, it would take place in the early hours before dawn. That was usually when violent death came. And as he patrolled, he thought of the Parkers. Tanner could almost hear the echoes of history as he trod across the land that once bore their name, and where generations of their family had lived and died.

After staying to the shadows cast by the nearby trees, Tanner crossed over to the porch and saw the figure seated in a wicker chair. It was Romina. She was crying softly, the sound like a whisper, when contrasted with the sonorous echo coming from the stable, as one of the horses snored in his sleep.

Tanner made a point of stepping on a section of the steps that he knew creaked. Romina looked over at him with a start, before wiping her eyes with a tissue she took from a pocket of her robe.

"Oh, Tanner, you scared me. What are you doing up?"

"Standing watch, just in case."

"All night?"

"Yeah, now tell me, what's got you crying?"

"My boyfriend, ex-boyfriend, Billy. I broke up with him today and he's been leaving me some really mean text messages since midnight. Well, some are mean, and then in others he begs me to give him another chance."

"And will you give him a second chance?"

"No, and Chaz Willis already asked me out. I said yes."

"Chaz, so he's named after his father?"

"Um-hmm, and he's so cute."

Tanner sat across from Romina. "Would you like some advice?"

"Yeah?"

"Stop reading the messages this Billy sends you. You broke up with him and that's that. Besides, don't you have to take a math test in a few hours?"

Romina yawned. "I do, trigonometry, and I'd better get some sleep. I'll also turn off my phone."

She rose from her seat and kissed Tanner on the cheek. "Goodnight, and you should get some sleep too."

"I caught a few hours earlier."

Romina looked out at the darkness. "Do you really think someone might try to hurt us?"

"I don't know, but if they come I'll be ready for them."

"Better safe than sorry, hmm?"

"Yes, better safe than sorry."

And Tanner knew from personal experience that sorry never went away.

He watched Romina return inside and then continued his night of vigilance.

20

SOMETIMES A ROCK IS ALL YOU NEED

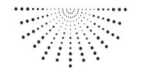

THE PARKER RANCH, SEPTEMBER 1997

They came just after three a.m. on a Saturday night.

All four men carried silenced Heckler & Koch MP5 submachine guns and were dressed in black.

They had parked their stolen vehicle at the mouth of the Parker driveway, and then walked in.

The home was dark and everyone inside was asleep. There had been a time, in decades past, when men, ranch employees, would have been asleep in the old bunkhouse, but that dilapidated structure had sat vacant for many years. The ranch hands all had homes of their own to go to when the day's work was done.

However, the Parkers did have at least one employee on site, and his name was Tanner. Tanner, who had been awake, had heard the car doors opening and closing, and had positioned himself behind a tree where the driveway began.

The four shapes gliding toward him looked like

shadows, and whatever they wore on their feet made very little sound as they moved across the gravel.

Tanner waited until they were ten yards away and opened fire with his .40 Smith & Wesson. The two men on the left went down with head wounds, then Tanner moved away just in time to avoid the barrage of bullets the other two men fired.

The *pff! pff! pff! pff! pff!* of their sound-suppressed shots was nearly as unnerving as the bullets themselves. Tanner knew these weren't cowboys from McKay's ranch, but professional killers like himself.

The remaining two men emerged from the driveway with each of them spraying bullets in a wide arc, three of which struck very close to Tanner, where he hid from sight behind the rear tire of Frank Parker's pickup truck.

Tanner fired again, and although it took several shots, he killed a third man. The remaining man closed in on his position, but Tanner had already sprinted for a new place to take cover, as the man's gun went dry.

He had been headed for a wide tree near the fence and away from the house, but the last man changed magazines so quickly that Tanner found himself forced to dive for cover behind a large wheelbarrow, which he tipped on its side.

It was damn poor cover, but the 9mm bullets did ping off the thick steel with a sound that reminded Tanner of a bell ringing.

He returned fire without hitting the man, then had to change the magazine in his own gun. As he did so, he heard the man sprinting his way while still firing.

One of the man's shots ricocheted off the lip of the wheelbarrow and just grazed Tanner's gun, causing him to fumble it. Tanner expected that at any moment the man would fire over the top of the wheelbarrow and blow him away.

A voice cried out from the barn and the man with the gun grunted, as a rock slammed into the side of his head, halting him for just a moment.

It was Pablo. He had awakened from the sound of Tanner's gun and gave aid with the only weapon he could find. Frank Parker had offered the boy his guest room, but Pablo refused and returned to the barn.

Tanner was happy he had done so, as his sudden appearance and audacious attack gave him the time he needed to reload. Tanner slammed the new magazine home and was ready to fire when a shot boomed from the bedroom window of Cody Parker. The round hit the last of Martillo's men square in the back, severing his spine and killing him.

Tanner looked up in time to see Cody slide down the roof of the porch and drop to the ground in a crouch at the side of the steps. Cody was barefoot and wearing only a pair of blue boxer shorts, however, his eyes were alert and his rifle ready.

"How many more?" Cody called to him.

Tanner stood. "Your man was the last, and thanks for that. I'm not sure I would have shot him in time. I also owe thanks to Pablo for giving me a chance to reload."

Cody came out of his crouch and saw the other man lying dead past the truck. "There were two of them?" Cody said, as Pablo came over to join them.

"Four," Tanner said. "I killed the first two while they were still coming down the driveway."

"I only heard one gun, and that ringing noise."

"Their weapons had suppressors; the damn things barely made a sound."

The front door flew open and Frank Parker stepped out

holding a large revolver. Like his son, he was dressed only in a pair of boxers. The sound of the baby crying carried from inside the house.

"Tanner, what's going on?"

"Four armed men attacked, Mr. Parker. But don't worry, they're all dead."

Parker spotted his son. "Are you all right? And how did you beat me downstairs?"

"I left by the window in my bedroom, and that last man over there was mine."

"But you're all right?"

"Yeah, Dad, I'm fine."

"How about Pablo there, and Tanner?"

"We're good, Frank," Tanner said, then he tousled Pablo's hair, causing the boy to grin. "And Pablo helped too. If he hadn't distracted that last shooter I might be dead."

"I'll go call the sheriff, and Tanner, thank you."

"You're welcome, but I don't think this is over. McKay is insane and needs to be put down."

Frank paused before entering the house.

"We'll talk later."

∽

THE SHERIFF SHOWED UP JUST BEFORE FOUR A.M.

He was out of uniform and wearing jeans that looked like they'd spent a week in a clothes hamper. His face grew paler with each body he viewed.

"These dudes are all Mexican by the look of them, and my brother doesn't have any damn Mexicans working for him."

"He hired them, just like he tried to hire me," Tanner said.

"That's a goddamn lie! I tell you my brother isn't fool enough to do something like this. Frank, you must have made another enemy somewhere, maybe a Mexican?"

"I have one enemy, Sheriff, and that's your brother. At least, he thinks he's my enemy. As far as I'm concerned the man can go to hell."

The sheriff waved his hands in the air as if to signal the end of the discussion. "Enough. My people will clean up this nightmare and then I'll post a deputy out front for the next few nights. After that, well, we'll see."

When the sheriff walked off, Cody shook his head. "Mr. McKay has to go, or we'll never be safe."

Tanner silently agreed, and while the sheriff had his deputy guarding the Parkers, Tanner planned to pay a visit to McKay and put an end to things, the law be damned.

"It'll all work out, Cody, trust me."

However, Tanner's words couldn't have been more wrong.

21

HOME IS WHERE THE HEART IS

The next "accident" at the Reyes Ranch occurred the following morning, when the housekeeper, Mrs. Salgado, opened a cabinet door and a butcher knife fell out and sliced open her forearm just above the wrist. The knife had been poised on a slanted cutting board in such a way as to make it fall. The cut was a deep gash that hit the vein and sent blood spurting.

Maria had been coming down the hall. After hearing the old woman cry out in shock and pain, she rushed into the kitchen.

"Madre de Dios!"

Maria grabbed a dish towel that was hanging nearby and tried to put pressure on the flow of blood. She cried out for someone to help while watching the white towel turn red.

Tanner and Doc rushed in from where they had been seated on the porch. Their guns were at the ready, but when Doc saw what was happening, he put his gun down, took off his belt, and wrapped it tightly around Mrs. Salgado's arm, which he elevated above her head.

The blood flow lessened immediately, and Doc used a second dishtowel to apply pressure to the cut.

Romina appeared wearing a blue bath towel. She had been in the shower when all the shouting started. Her hair still dripped shampoo. When she was told what had happened to Mrs. Salgado, she looked over at the cabinet with a puzzled expression.

"How could that happen?"

"I was wondering the same thing," Tanner said, as he dialed for an ambulance.

Mrs. Salgado, with her face looking very pale, murmured that it was an accident. However, the knife had fallen from the cabinet above the stove, when it should have been in its slot inside the knife set on the counter.

∽

BEFORE SHE CLIMBED ABOARD THE AMBULANCE TO RIDE TO the hospital with Mrs. Salgado, Maria gave Doc a hug.

"Oh, thank God you were here, or I think she might have bled to death."

"I was happy to help," Doc said.

Maria smiled. "You have a job here if you still want it. Hopefully, I won't need security much longer, but there's always work that needs doing."

Doc grinned. "Yes ma'am. That sounds fine."

Maria climbed aboard the ambulance and Tanner watched it drive off, as Romina and Doc stood beside him. Romina had changed into her clothes, but still needed to do her hair, which was hidden beneath a kerchief. When she checked her phone, she looked startled.

"Oh, look at the time; I have to leave for school soon."

"I'll be here when you're ready, and we'll stop and get you breakfast on the way," Tanner said.

"Okay."

Romina took two steps, but she came back and kissed Doc on the cheek. "You're not too old, and you're my hero for saving Mrs. Salgado."

Doc watched her go with a smile on his face. "That girl is gold, and nothing like that brother of hers. By the way, where is he?"

"He left out of here just after first light," Tanner said.

"The kid is lazy, seems like all he does is sit in that room of his and play video games, that is, when he's not off riding that motorcycle."

"I'm going to run a little errand today and won't be back right away."

"Where are you going?"

"I'm going to locate the Harvey brothers and find out what they know. If that knife had hit the old woman's throat, she'd be dead. And it could just have easily been Romina who opened that cabinet."

"You want me to come with you? I'm not much with a gun, but I could back you up."

"Thanks, but I'll go alone. Things could get... messy."

"I hear you, and speaking of messes, I'll clean up the kitchen and put on a pot of coffee for when Maria gets back."

"It looks like you've found a home here."

"You could probably make one here too if you wanted to."

"What?"

"A home, you could probably make a home here too."

"Home," Tanner said, and as he looked around, his mind traveled backwards in time, to when the land he stood upon was owned by the Parkers, and he became lost in thought.

"Tanner?"

Tanner snapped out of his reverie and was surprised to see Romina standing before him.

"Are you okay?" she asked.

"I'm fine, are you ready?"

"Um-hmm, bye Doc."

"Have a good day at school, sweetie, and Tanner, take care."

Tanner drove away from the ranch with the girl, Romina, seated beside him, but it was a boy named Cody Parker that rode along with him, and who would stay with him the rest of his life.

22
MANY PAWNS

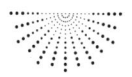

THE MCKAY RANCH, SEPTEMBER 1997

After learning about the slaughter of Martillo's men, Jack Sheer informed McKay that there would be consequences. After contacting Martillo by phone using a number he'd been given, they learned how expensive those consequences would be.

McKay leaned over his desk and glared at Sheer, who sat in a chair in front of it with his crutches leaning against his legs. The two men had been in San Antonio so they would have an alibi, only to return and find that things didn't go as planned.

"A hundred grand? Is this beaner insane?"

"Two of the men that died were his nephews, but on the bright side, he now wants the Parkers dead more than you do."

"Big deal. That's what I paid him for. If this Martillo asshole thinks I'm paying him another cent, he can go fuck himself."

"I know it's a lot of money, but Martillo, he's part of a cartel down there. Andy, those bastards don't mess around."

"Cartel? So what? This is America. I'll be damned if I'm going to pay a man more money for screwing up a job. Those men that got killed must not have been very good. If he wants to send more of those losers against me, let him, I'll have a dozen men guarding me at all times."

"That's expensive."

"Hell yeah, but it don't cost a hundred grand, and if he does attack, it'll make me look innocent of the attack on Parker."

"You really want me to tell him no?"

McKay grabbed the receiver off the phone on his desk, but then remembered that phone records could be traced.

"Go back into town and make the call. Tell that bastard that I said he can fuck himself."

Sheer let out a sigh, stood with the aid of his crutches, and grabbed his hat off the desk.

"I think you're making a mistake, but you're the boss."

"Damn right I am. And send Whit in here. I'll have him and some of the boys work overtime as guards starting tonight. If that Mex tries anything, we'll be ready."

~

Sheer cursed and then winced in pain, as he accidentally slammed the door of the phone booth on his cast. When he was finally settled inside the cramp enclosure, he took the strip of paper with the phone number from his pocket and dialed the bar in Mexico. He had filled his pockets with change before leaving the ranch, but the call still ate up most of it and only a quarter remained by the time he finished feeding the phone.

The money bought him three minutes of talk time. He grew nervous when two minutes passed and Martillo had still not come on the line. But with less than thirty seconds left, he heard a scraping sound, as if the phone was being moved across a surface. It was followed by Martillo's soft voice.

"Jack, what answer does your king have for me?"

"He won't pay. He says it's not his fault that your men failed."

"I will come with many pawns, Jack, and the board will be swept clean."

"This isn't me, Martillo, you know? You and I are still cool."

"You're a pawn, Jack. If you stand near your king, you'll leave the board too."

There was a click and the phone went dead.

Sheer took the final quarter from his pocket and fed it into the phone. After a few seconds, McKay answered his call.

"Andy, about those guards, you might want to add as many as you can; Martillo is definitely coming."

"Let him come," McKay snarled, and afterwards, Sheer heard the phone slam down.

He stood inside the phone booth with its little fan whirring overhead above its dim light. Two words kept passing through his mind.

Many pawns.

Sheer sighed in resignation to his fate, then left the booth to return to his king's side.

23

HARD OR EASY?

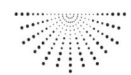

Tanner found the Harvey brothers sitting inside their truck outside Stark Lake Park. After watching them for only a few minutes, he could tell they were selling pot.

The law enforcement in the town was never good, and it looked like the tradition continued. Either that, or the cops that patrolled the park were being paid to look the other way.

Stark Lake Park was a new addition to the town since Tanner had last been there. It was only about twelve acres of land, while the lake was man-made and about four times the size of a swimming pool. However, there was a running track, along with basketball and tennis courts.

The Harvey brothers were situated on a corner with a line of parked cars behind them. When Tanner pulled his pickup truck in front of them on an angle, the boys were essentially blocked in. Tanner reached the driver's side window before either of them could react.

"Relax, all I want is information."

"Fuck you," Rich said, as Ernie gazed at him with fear in his eyes, while remembering how it felt not to be able to breathe. Tanner saw that Ernie's throat was still bruised from where he had struck him.

"You can tell me what I want to know, or you can play dumb. If you play dumb, I'll come at you again when you're not expecting it, then I'll ask my questions in a way you won't like. What's it going to be?"

Rich glared at him, but Ernie spoke up. "What do you want to know?"

"Who hired you to intimidate the Reyes family?"

"It was the kid."

"What kid?"

"You know, Javier, Javier Reyes."

"Javier hired you to give his own mother grief?"

Rich spoke up. "It probably wasn't his idea. He runs with those motorcycle punks. All I know is that he paid us two bills a day to run off anybody looking for work there."

"Where did he get the money? Is he selling drugs?"

"Those dudes, they transport, but not here, they do a little business up in San Antonio, but they're nothing."

"What's the name of the gang?"

Rich laughed. "You know how those pricks roll. The name probably has the word devil or diablo in it somewhere, but they hang out over by the railroad tracks on the other side of Highway 16. It's a place that used to be a Taco Queen."

"You're not still working for him, are you?"

"No, man. It sucked sitting out on that road all day. At least when we're here we get to see some ladies jogging by."

"And nobody kicks your ass."

"That too, so are we done?"

"We're done. But if I see you at the Reyes Ranch again you won't like what comes next."

"Yeah, tough guy, we hear you. Hey, you want to buy some weed? We got good shit."

"Maybe next time."

Tanner drove away from the park, but he had more questions than when he'd arrived there.

24

A RAT ABANDONS HIS SHIP

THE MCKAY RANCH, SEPTEMBER 1997

Tanner had traveled on foot to kill McKay and found that the man had upped his security considerably.

There were two armed guards doing crisscrossing circuits around the ranch house, while four stood on the porch holding rifles, and two more guarded the entrance to the driveway.

Tanner moved closer to the house by staying in the shadows and hunkered down at the base of a wide tree, which was twenty feet from the home.

Beyond the house, light spilled from the stables, and Tanner heard several voices amid the clinking of what sounded like poker chips. That meant there would be still more men to deal with.

The level of security puzzled Tanner.

If McKay was expecting an attack, then why not involve his brother the sheriff and have deputies guarding him, such as the one assigned to guard the entrance to the Parker ranch.

By not involving the law, it meant that McKay was hiding something from his brother. Tanner could guess what that something was.

The shooters had all been Mexican and were affiliated with a gang in Mexico that was known to be involved in the drug trade as security for couriers.

McKay must have hired those men to kill the Parkers, and their employers weren't happy about losing four soldiers.

Tanner smirked. McKay's insane quest for vengeance had made him a bigger target for revenge than the Parkers had ever been.

A door at the side of the house opened and Jack Sheer hobbled out on his crutches. Sheer was dragging a big duffel bag behind him, the type that had a thick strap so you could sling it across your back.

After looking about to see if anyone was watching, Sheer headed toward a car parked near the door. After some difficulty, due to his bad foot and the size of the huge green bag, Sheer managed to wedge the duffel inside the trunk.

One of the guards came around the corner of the house and called to Sheer, just as the ranch foreman slammed the lid on the trunk shut.

"Jack!"

Tanner saw Sheer nearly jump out of his skin and knew the man was up to something. If the guard noticed, he hadn't let on, and smiled as he approached Sheer. The guard was young, about Tanner's age, with straw-colored hair and a big gap-toothed grin.

"What's up, Jack?"

"Nothing, Ray, how are things with you?"

"I'm liking this easy overtime with another baby on the way, but what do you think the odds are that we'll see any trouble?"

Sheer said nothing, but Tanner saw that his right hand had begun to twitch.

"Jack?"

"Um, no trouble. This is just a precaution because a deal that Mr. McKay was involved in went wrong. Besides, if anything happens the boss can always call in his brother the sheriff, right?"

The guard, Ray, seemed to relax at those words.

"Yeah, that's right, the cops will back us up. What kind of people was the boss dealing with?"

"Legitimate, or so he thought, until the man threatened him on the phone."

Ray shook his head sadly. "It takes all kinds, but that's enough yakking. I have to keep moving or the other perimeter guard, Ed, will report me. You know what a prick that guy is."

"Right, see you around, Ray."

When the guard was out of sight, Sheer opened the car door to get in, but then banged a fist on the roof of the vehicle while muttering something to himself, as if recalling that he'd forgotten something.

After watching him hobble back inside the house, Tanner saw the second guard appear. The man came from the opposite direction that the first one had. After watching the man until he rounded a corner of the house, Tanner left the shadows and went to the car, where he reached in and pulled on the trunk release lever.

Tanner removed the duffel bag from the trunk and sat it by the door, behind a large bush. He then climbed inside the trunk, but only after he pulled back the carpet to uncover the cable that controlled the trunk release, so he wouldn't be trapped inside.

He had his gun ready in case Sheer opened the trunk again, but doubted that he would do so, since the duffel bag had to be wedged inside and had taken up all the space.

Twenty seconds after lowering the trunk lid, Tanner could hear Sheer approaching in that faltering gait that the crutches gave him.

The motor started, just after the front end of the car lowered from Sheer's weight in the driver's seat, and soon they were on the move.

Once Tanner had Sheer away from the ranch and without the guards to intervene, he would get answers from the man. He would also teach him the price for not heeding his warning, a warning he delivered when he shot him in the foot.

Tanner was young, and he had discovered that those older often discounted him because of his youth. But Sheer would learn the folly of such thinking. It would be the last lesson he would ever learn.

Within minutes, Sheer was motoring along on Highway 16, and Tanner settled in for the ride.

25

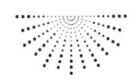

ME FIRST

Tanner felt an unfamiliar twinge of concern for another human being the moment he heard what had happened. Romina was missing.

After a polite, if strained, meeting with Maria at the ranch, when Chaz Willis came by to pick up Romina for their date, the two teens left in his car and headed to the movies. Chaz was seventeen, tall, dark, and as good-looking as his father. He spoke politely to Maria and appeared to adore Romina, who was smiling at everything the boy said. She looked as happy as Tanner had ever seen her.

Tanner had wanted to follow, just in case, but both Romina and Maria told him it wouldn't be necessary. Tanner stayed behind and lay down for a nap before he rose to begin his usual nightly vigil.

Doc shook him awake less than three hours later. That was when Tanner learned that Chaz had called the house asking to speak to Romina, who he believed had abandoned him at the movie theater. After Maria told Chaz that Romina hadn't come back home, she discovered that her daughter's phone wasn't being answered. Maria had asked Doc to get Tanner.

Tanner found her standing outside. She was staring at the driveway as if she were willing Romina to appear.

"I don't know what to do," Maria said, and Tanner saw that her eyes were on the verge of tears.

Javier was present as well and looked numb with worry for his sister.

Maria let loose a long sigh. "I called the police and they said it was too soon to panic. I understand that, but with everything else that's been going on around here, I just… oh God, where is she? I called her friends, and no one knows anything. I even tried Tonya Jennings, wondering if she had gone to see her, but no, no one knows where she is."

Headlights came down the drive and Chaz Willis's car appeared. When he climbed out of it, the kid looked both bewildered and scared, as he approached the group and explained what had happened.

"When the movie ended, we both had to use the bathroom, so I went into the men's room while Romina walked toward the ladies' room on the other side of the lobby. When I came out, I walked over there and waited, but after fifteen minutes went by, I started to worry. That's when I asked a girl I know from school to check and see if Romina was inside, and she said that she wasn't."

"What did you do then?" Tanner asked.

"I looked everywhere for her and kept calling her phone. I thought we were having a great time, but now I don't know. I thought maybe she dropped out of the date for some reason… and that's when I called here."

Another set of headlights came down the driveway and Tonya appeared. She walked over to Maria and took her hand.

"Is there any word yet?"

Maria shook her head, and this time a tear fell. She looked over at Chaz with pleading eyes.

"Have you done something to my daughter? Is your father behind this?"

Chaz looked taken aback by the accusations, as well as insulted. "Mrs. Reyes, I would never hurt Romina, and neither would my father."

"I have an idea," Tanner said. "Maria, where does Romina's ex-boyfriend live?"

"Billy? Do you think he's done something to her?"

"I don't know, but I'll find out."

"I know where Billy lives," Chaz said.

Tanner joined him in his car, as Maria joined Tonya in hers to follow. Doc and Javier stayed behind in case Romina came home.

Chaz gripped the steering wheel tightly as he drove, and his handsome young face twisted into a grimace filled with hate.

"If that fucking Billy has hurt Romina, I'll kill him, I swear I will."

"You'll have to get in line," Tanner said, as he touched the knife in his pocket.

26
A WASTE OF A GOOD ROOM

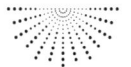

SOMEWHERE NORTH OF SAN ANTONIO, TEXAS, SEPTEMBER 1997

AFTER MORE THAN AN HOUR HAD PASSED, TANNER BEGAN to think that stowing away inside Sheer's trunk wasn't such a good idea after all.

When the car finally came to a stop five minutes later, Tanner felt the car rise, as Sheer removed his bulk from the vehicle. Tanner gripped his gun tightly, while waiting for the trunk to open.

The trunk lid stayed closed and a scraping sound came, as Sheer slid the nozzle of a gas pump into the opening on the side of the car.

Within minutes, they were back on the road. It was another half an hour until Sheer stopped again and left the car. Tanner took a chance and pulled on the cable that controlled the trunk release. It took much more effort than using the latch inside the car, but after three seconds of steady pulling, the trunk unlatched and popped open partway.

They were at a motel that was set off a highway. After verifying that no one was in sight other than the people in the passing cars, Tanner stepped out of the trunk and felt his cramped legs and back sigh with relief. Before closing the lid, he covered up the release cable with the carpet again, then secured the trunk lid shut as quietly as he could.

The car was parked just to the right of the window that looked into the motel office. Tanner saw that Sheer was taking a room, as the middle-aged motel manager handed a key across the counter.

The woman pointed to her left, likely indicating to Sheer where his room was located. Tanner moved in that direction before Sheer could turn around. He was at the ice machine and facing away when Sheer backed the car into the slot before Room 12.

Sheer hobbled around on his crutches to the rear of the vehicle just as a young couple was walking by. The woman was a blonde wearing a short dress. After saying hello to the couple, Sheer watched the woman until she and her boyfriend entered their room, which was two doors down from Sheer's.

Tanner used this distraction to ease closer, and when Sheer opened the trunk with his key, Tanner was standing right behind him.

Sheer whispered, "What the hell?" as he stared into the empty trunk.

Tanner gave out a little whistle, and Sheer nearly fell as he spun to face him on his crutches.

"Tanner?"

After ripping the car keys out of Sheer's hand, Tanner gripped the crutches and kicked Sheer in his ample gut.

That caused the ranch foreman to fall on his ass inside the trunk, while also banging his head on the rim of the trunk lid.

"We need to talk," Tanner said. He shoved Sheer's legs inside the trunk and closed it on him. Twenty seconds later, Tanner had the car back on the highway and was searching for a secluded spot.

Back at the motel, the crutches laid discarded on the ground. Sheer would soon have no need of them, or of anything else in this world, and he would tell Tanner everything he wanted to know.

27
DRAGON SLAYER

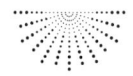

Romina's ex-boyfriend, Billy, lived in a quiet neighborhood of new two-story homes.

Each home had a driveway on the left and a deck in the rear, but no basement. With the house shrouded in darkness, Tanner feared that the boy may have taken her somewhere else.

That is, if Billy was even the one who took Romina.

It briefly crossed Tanner's mind that the Harvey brothers might have grabbed her, but he dismissed the idea. That level of escalation didn't seem like something they would have the balls for. Also, they would have to know that he would kill them once he found them.

Romina likely accompanied the person who had her on her own or was tricked by them. She wouldn't trust the Harvey brothers enough for either scenario to play out.

Tonya parked her car behind Chaz's, and Tanner and Chaz walked back to speak to her and Maria, as Tonya lowered her window.

"You two stay here while I check out the house."

"It looks like no one is at home," Maria said, but Chaz

pointed to the car that he had parked behind, an old Chevy.

"I'm not 100% sure, but I think that's Billy's car."

"Everybody wait here," Tanner said. "I'm going to check out that car and then the house."

"I'm coming with you," Chaz said.

"That's not a good idea, kid."

"I wasn't asking," Chaz said, and Tanner nodded, liking the boy's fire.

"Let's go."

When they reached the car, Chaz let out a little moan after looking inside.

"That green sweater on the back seat there, Romina was wearing that inside the theater because of the air-conditioning."

Tanner recognized the sweater as well, and when he peered down the driveway, he saw a narrow strip of light coming out from beneath the garage door.

"Stay behind me," he told Chaz, then he walked toward the garage.

As they drew closer, they could hear a male voice that sounded plaintive in tone, but couldn't make out the words. Once there, Tanner tried the door handle very gently and discovered that it was locked. He then eased around to a window on the side and peered in through a gap on the right, at the edge of the curtains.

Romina was seated in a wooden chair at the back left-hand corner of the garage. She was tearful and frightened. She appeared to be unharmed, but her ankles were duct taped to the chair legs while her wrists were similarly bound to the arms.

Seated and facing her in a matching chair was a boy with blond hair that fell past his shoulders. He was wearing a long-sleeved dress shirt and pants from a suit. The boy was pleading with Romina while one hand gestured wildly and the other hung limp and held a gun.

Chaz whispered, "Oh shit," when he spotted the gun. Tanner gestured for him to remain quiet, before taking the boy by the arm and pulling him away from the garage.

"Go to Miss Jennings and have her call the cops. If Billy's parents come home or if anybody else tries to come back here, stop them, especially Maria, Mrs. Reyes. The last thing we want to do is panic Billy."

"All right, but what are you going to do?"

Tanner brought out his gun. "I'm going to free Romina."

Chaz looked at the gun and then up into Tanner's eyes. "Are you going to kill him?"

"We'll see. But Romina is coming out of there alive, I promise you that. And one more thing, I'll need the keys to your car."

Chaz hesitated for just an instant before handing Tanner the keys. While Chaz walked over to talk to Tonya and Maria, Tanner started Chaz's car. While keeping the lights off, he turned into the driveway, cut the engine, and let the vehicle coast toward the garage. Once there, he restarted the engine, turned on the high beams, and blasted the radio.

He was out of the car and standing at the side of the garage door when it went up three feet. Billy ducked beneath it, before letting the door fall shut behind him. Tanner watched as Billy shielded his eyes with his hands and saw that he had tucked the gun behind his back in his waistband.

"Who's there?"

Tanner fought the urge to shoot the little psycho. Instead, he just reached over and removed Billy's gun, which caused the kid to spin around and face him, while crying out in surprise.

"Hey!"

Tanner smashed Billy across the face with an elbow and Billy's hands flew to his broken nose. Tanner then kicked him in the balls, grabbed him by the hair, and kneed him in the side of the head for good measure.

Billy collapsed to the ground with a moan, and Tanner raised the door and stepped inside the garage.

"Tanner!" Romina said, as he drew closer. Until that moment, she had been so blinded by the headlights that all she saw were shadows.

Tanner freed her by using his knife, and Romina hugged him fiercely.

"Oh, thank God, I thought he might kill me."

"You're safe," Tanner said, as he felt feelings he thought were long dead. It was a need to protect, and he knew that if something had happened to this girl that he would not have forgiven himself for failing her.

After hugging her back, he pried her loose and spoke. "Did he rape you?"

"No, he just kept begging me to take him back. I think he's high on something, maybe heroin."

"Your mother is out front with Chaz and Miss Jennings, go see her."

Romina pointed at Billy, who had made it to his hands and knees, but looked as if he might puke.

"What about him?"

"I'll stay with him until the police come."

Romina eased past Billy as if he were toxic, and then she ran down the driveway toward her mother.

Tanner turned off Chaz's car, killed the lights, and helped Billy over to the chair that Romina had been strapped into.

"Look at me, kid."

Billy did so, and Tanner could see that he had broken his nose, while the left side of Billy's face was already beginning to swell.

"I want you to listen to me and I want you to hear me."

Tanner jammed Billy's own gun into the boy's mouth with so much force that it chipped one of the kid's teeth and cut the roof of his mouth.

"You are going to plead guilty to every charge. You will plead as an adult and you will serve every last day of your sentence. I don't care what your parents want. I don't care what your lawyer may say, but you'll confess to your crimes in writing. You'll do your time, and you'll stay away from Romina. If you fail to do what I'm telling you, I will kill you. Do you understand me?"

Billy stared at Tanner with wide eyes and nodded as best as he could, with the gun jammed in his mouth.

Tanner searched the boy's eyes, then grimaced, while guessing that there was a chance he'd have to kill the little turd someday. If he weren't so tied in with the Reyes family, Billy would be dead already, kid or not.

Tanner stood and put away the gun, as Billy spit out bits of tooth and gagged on his own blood.

The cops were coming, and Tanner would have to talk to them.

Tim assured Tanner that the fake ID he sent him would pass scrutiny. Tanner was about to put it to the test.

Billy began sobbing and Tanner walked over and sat on the hood of Chaz's car, just as Tonya appeared. She took one look at Billy and shook her head in disgust.

"You hurt him, good!"

"Yes."

"Given the chance, I might have killed him," she said, and Tanner heard the anger in her voice.

"I still might," Tanner said, and saw Billy flinch.

Tonya walked around until she was standing before Tanner, then she leaned forward and kissed him. Tanner took her in his arms, and to his surprise, she didn't back away.

"What was that kiss for?"

"For saving the damsel in distress."

"I fight dragons too."

Tonya laughed. "I'm sure you do."

Blue and red lights filled the night. The cops had arrived.

Tonya stepped back as she sent Tanner a smile. "To be continued."

She then went off to speak to the cops.

"Billy?" Tanner said.

Billy answered in a nasal tone, due to his broken nose, which had already swollen.

"I believe you, man… I saw it in your eyes."

"If you're lying, someday they'll be the last thing you see."

Tonya returned with two cops and a long night became longer.

28

THEY'RE COMING

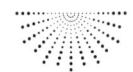

SOMEWHERE NORTHWEST OF SAN ANTONIO, TEXAS, SEPTEMBER 1997

Tanner bumped the car slowly along a rutted road then killed the engine, before walking around to the trunk and opening it.

Sheer gazed up at him with wild eyes and held up a hand as if he could block bullets with it. "Don't kill me!"

Tanner put the gun away, reached down, and dragged Sheer out of the trunk and onto the ground.

Sheer whimpered in pain, because his damaged foot had slammed against the lip of the trunk.

They were down an old unused patch of broken asphalt that at one time must have been a road. It was in a strip of desert two miles from the highway. Tanner shut the trunk and sat on it, as he asked his first question.

"Why does McKay have so many men around?"

"It's ah, it's for Parker and you. He was afraid that you would try to kill him."

Tanner got off the trunk and kicked Sheer in the face hard enough to send him rolling away. If McKay was afraid of Frank Parker, he'd have cops around, but he didn't want cops around, because they might start asking questions.

"The truth, or I have no use for you."

Sheer took a minute to recover as he spat out the blood that was filling his mouth. After touching a loose tooth with the tip of his tongue, he answered the question.

"Martillo. He's part of a Mexican cartel and he's the one who sent those men to Parker's ranch."

"Martillo means hammer. Is that really his name?"

"No, but he sometimes kills with a hammer, and you know how that goes, the name stuck. Now Martillo is pissed that his men are dead, and he blames McKay."

"How did McKay contact him, and don't lie."

"It was me. I knew Martillo from the old days, but he's moved up inside the cartel. Now I'm not sure what he'll do, but I wasn't sticking around to find out and—where's my duffel bag?"

"I tossed it out at the ranch."

"Shit, all my stuff was in there, and money too, almost five grand."

Tanner wasn't listening anymore, as a thought came to him. "This Martillo, how many men will he send to kill McKay?"

"I don't know, but it will be a shitload more than the four pawns he sent last time."

"Pawns?"

Sheer explained about Martillo's code talk and then began rambling about the first time he'd met him. He was trying to buy time to delay what he knew was coming.

Tanner asked a question and cut him off. "When will Martillo come?"

"Any day now; it's why I got out of there. I tried to talk sense into Andy, but he won't take Martillo seriously, and Martillo's no joke."

"You're right," Tanner said, while wondering if the sheriff's deputy parked outside the Parker Ranch would be enough to turn Martillo away once he killed McKay.

He doubted it. What's the death of one cop after you've just slaughtered over a dozen men?

Sheer was just able to say the words, "No, don't—" before Tanner shot him twice in the head and left him to rot in the desert.

He had to get back to the Parker Ranch before it was too late. As he drove along, he did something he hadn't done since he was a child.

He prayed.

29
NO APPEALS

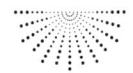

The Taco Queen in the neighboring town of Culver looked as if it had been closed for years. Graffiti and gang signs marred its formerly white exterior.

With Romina back home and safe, Tanner decided to have a look at what was reportedly the hangout of the motorcycle gang Javier belonged to.

After leaving the pickup truck in the parking lot of a diner, Tanner walked across desert scrubland and approached the old Taco Queen building from the rear.

No one was in the area except those passing by in cars on the road in front. The back door of the Taco Queen had been kicked in long ago, so Tanner entered and looked around.

The place was a mess, and food containers and pizza cartons littered the floor. There was one area near the boarded-up front windows that was cleared of debris and had a table and chairs set up inside it.

Tanner looked down at the tabletop and saw magazines that were about guns, drug paraphernalia, and motorcycles. All of them had beautiful women showing lots of skin on every cover. Sex sells.

There was a denim vest draped over one of the chairs, it had a patch that showed a grinning skull and the words Diablo Boys. Rich Harvey had been right; the club's name did contain the word Diablo.

The building had a large storage area inside that had once been a freezer, but all the components had been removed when the place shut down. Anything of value, such as the copper tubing, had been stripped by someone and sold as scrap metal.

There was a large, crude bulls-eye spray-painted on the rear wall of the freezer, and over a hundred rounds had perforated it, while 9mm shell casings decorated the floor. Tanner marveled at the stupidity.

Granted, the sheet metal comprising the rear wall was thin, but the cinder block behind it wasn't. The wall could have easily sent a ricocheting round back toward the person who fired it. Add to that the fact that the building had steel frame construction, and the gang's firing range could be a death trap if a bullet struck one of the steel girders.

A rumbling noise reached Tanner's ears. The Diablo Boys had returned. Earlier, Tanner had looked inside an empty storage closet that was on the left side, near where the counter once stood. That was where he decided to go, so that he could listen in on them and maybe discover what was going on.

Before stepping into the storage closet, he watched as five motorcycles drove around to the rear and parked. Javier Reyes was riding on the last bike. He was the only one that wasn't wearing a T-shirt or jacket with the gang's insignia.

Tanner also saw that the boy wasn't wearing his

helmet, but had it strapped down behind him. Apparently, he only carried it around so that his mother wouldn't worry, but he kept it off to appear more macho in front of the gang.

Tanner stepped inside the closet and left the door cracked just enough to see out, as the first of the men walked inside, past his position, and plopped into a seat at the head of the table. The guy had a name stitched over the pocket of his vest which Tanner at first thought said Jeff, but then he squinted and could see that it read, Jefe', as in boss. How original.

The other men followed and took seats, all but Javier, who Tanner assumed was made to stand because he wasn't yet a member.

The other four men all looked alike, mid to late-thirties, with faded denim clothes, worn boots, and scruffy beards, but the one at the head of the table, Jefe', was a head taller than the others and the most muscular.

Jefe' gazed around the large room with contempt on his face. "Look at this shithole. How much longer do we have to stay here, Javier?"

Javier mumbled something that Tanner couldn't make out, nor could the gang's leader, as his next words indicated.

"Speak up! What excuse do you have now?"

"I said it's that guy, Tanner. He ran off the Harvey brothers and even took my mother to see Willis."

Tanner raised an eyebrow at the mention of Willis's name and wondered if maybe he was involved somehow.

"What happened?" Jefe' asked.

"Nothing. My mother still blames Willis for everything."

"Good, but you have to make your move soon, son, and didn't you say that Tanner dude was still there?"

"Yeah, the asshole wants to move in as far as I can tell."

"It don't matter. He was there when you rigged that knife to fall and he won't be able to stop this either."

Javier nodded, but shuffled his feet. "Isn't there some other way?"

Jefe' stood. When he walked over to Javier, Tanner saw the boy flinch, but Jefe' smiled and placed a muscular arm across Javier's shoulders, then he spoke to him in a fatherly manner.

"I know it won't be easy, but once it's done, you're in. You'll be one of us and everything gets made new. Then we can leave this shithole behind and start making some fat dollars, you hear me?"

"Yeah, I hear you."

"Do it tonight and it'll all work out, you'll see."

Javier reached in his pocket and removed a small bottle that held a yellowish powder.

"You're sure it's painless?"

"Absolutely, and there's no way to tie it back to you. Hey, you don't want us to have to do it, do you?"

Javier shook his head vigorously.

Jefe' took Javier by the shoulders and turned to speak to the other bikers. "Look at this guy. He's making moves like a man. The next time we see him, he'll be one of us."

The men cheered Javier and told him he was taking control of his life the way a man should, and then Jefe' slapped him on the back.

"Go home, act like everything's cool, and do what you got to do. I have faith in you, son. You're the future of the Diablo Boys."

Javier said goodbye, and seconds later, Tanner heard his bike start up, and then the sound faded as he rode off.

Jefe' returned to the table and the man at his right asked a question.

"Do you think he'll really do it?"

"Yeah, I do. He did everything else I asked. The little shit wants to be one of us and he knows that this is the only way that happens."

"That's one dumb motherfucker," one of the other men said. "Once we move in there, I'm gonna get real friendly with his sister. The girl is fine. I bet I can turn her out and have her doing blowjobs for twenty bucks, or maybe I'll just make her my bitch."

The other men laughed along with their friend, but the laughter died when Tanner stepped from the closet and shot the man in the back of the head. He killed a second man by the time the other two reacted. They dived beneath the table while reaching for their guns.

Tanner sent two shots through the tabletop to kill the third man, before Jefe' could clear his weapon, then Tanner told Jefe' that he wanted to see his hands.

As Jefe' raised his hands up, Tanner saw a wet spot spread across the tough guy's jeans.

"What is Javier supposed to do tonight?"

"You're... you're Tanner, aren't you?"

Tanner fired a bullet that hit Jefe' in the left shoulder.

"Answer my question."

Jefe' did answer the question, and several more after that, before Tanner left the leader of the Diablo Boys with a bullet in his head. He was tired of playing bodyguard and it felt good to kill.

Killing was something he had always understood. It was final. It offered no appeals, no plea-bargaining, and no second chances, and second chances were something that Tanner normally didn't grant. The gifting of one to Romina's crazed ex-boyfriend had put him in a bad mood.

He was determined to keep the Reyes family safe, and after learning the truth about Javier, he now knew that the real threat had been coming from within all along, and that Willis must have just been a convenient scapegoat.

Tanner wondered if Javier was a cancer that could be treated, or if he had to be cut out with a knife.

In either event, the Reyes family was in for grief, but at least two of them would still be alive when it was all over. That was more than could be said for the Parkers.

Tanner strode back to the pickup truck he'd left at the diner, ditched the gun in a dumpster, and drove back toward the ranch. As he did so, thoughts of the past filled his mind once more.

30

MASSACRE

THE MCKAY RANCH, SEPTEMBER 1997

THE BIG RED TRACTOR-TRAILER CAME TO A HALT JUST PAST the driveway, and the two ranch hands stationed there, men that McKay had turned into guards, assumed the driver would get out and ask them for directions.

When the driver did approach, he held a Heckler & Koch MP5 submachine gun with a sound suppressor attached. He emptied the entire thirty-round magazine into the two men and watched as they fell to the ground dead.

With the guards at the entrance eliminated, the man unlatched the rear doors of the truck and swung them open, so that twenty of the forty men aboard could get out and head for the ranch. Each man held his own MP5.

With half of his cargo delivered, the driver got back in the truck and moved along the three miles separating the McKay Ranch from the Parker Ranch. He drove with the rear doors still opened and secured, as the remaining men in the back held onto straps fastened to the wall. They sat atop crude benches made from wooden planks.

Once they'd arrived at the entrance to the Parker Ranch, the driver eased the truck around the police car and slowed to park. When the men at the rear of the truck spotted the cop inside the cruiser, they opened up on him, shredding both the man and the vehicle with over a hundred rounds.

The silenced guns worked so efficiently that death was delivered in an eerie muffled violence, which sounded something like a hundred people all spitting at once. If not for the discordant sounds of breaking glass and rending metal accompanied by the officer's screams, the death and destruction would have seemed surreal.

The remaining twenty men disembarked and joined the driver, who was already headed down the Parker's driveway.

The driver's name was Martillo, and tonight his cargo was death.

∼

THE FOUR MEN STANDING GUARD ON MCKAY'S PORCH DIED before they could ever give voice to warn the other men on the property, but no warning was needed, as bullets shredded everything in sight. Only the dead could have missed the fact that they were under attack.

Martillo's men spread out and kept firing, as they reloaded their weapons repeatedly. The attack was so devastating that McKay's men only got off five shots and caused only one injury.

In less than a minute, the home resembled a cheese grater, as over a thousand rounds perforated the structure to pass through furniture, inner walls, and people.

By the time Martillo's men had finished reloading for the fourth time, the baffles inside the sound suppressors began to fail, and the volume of the shots grew much louder.

McKay had stood up behind his desk at the beginning of the assault and wondered what was causing the screams and odd sounds he was hearing. Then several of Martillo's men reached the side of the home. When their silenced rounds entered McKay's office, he finally realized he was under attack.

After a round hit him in the left thigh, McKay fell to the floor and was showered by glass, as the large picture window behind him shattered. Although he was wounded, cut, and bleeding, McKay was able to reach up and grab his gun from off the desk.

He crawled across his office floor amid debris from the splintered walls and shelves and ran smack-dab into two of Martillo's soldiers in the doorway. Their weapons were aimed at his face.

McKay dropped his puny revolver and begged for his life. "Don't shoot! I'll pay! Oh Lord, don't shoot. I'll pay triple, I'll—"

The two men emptied their guns into McKay, then one of them spoke into a radio.

The gunfire outside grew sporadic before finally ceasing, and after looting the home of anything of value that they could carry, one of the men set the charge. The bomb he was preparing had been stolen from a military truck and was of an incendiary nature. It was a bomb designed to burn illegal crops, such as marijuana and opium poppy plants. It could defoliate up to twenty acres. Inside the confines of the McKay ranch house, it would burn everything to ash.

With the charge set to detonate, the men left the

McKay land in the vehicles of the men they had just killed and headed for the Parker Ranch to join their brothers.

They were an overwhelming force intent on slaughter and revenge, and on this night, they would have both.

The bomb exploded when they were a mile away, and the flash of the explosion could be seen.

When they heard the booming sound of a rifle coming from the Parker Ranch at their approach, they looked at each other in amazement that the fight was still going on. They would later learn that eight of their fellows had perished before their arrival, and that a sixteen-year-old boy had killed them.

Cody Parker was the last man standing, and he was determined to kill them all.

Alas, it was not to be.

~

Tanner was pushing Sheer's car to its limit as he sped back to the Parker Ranch. He had a bad feeling in his gut that was increasing with each passing second.

His lone hope was that the presence of a police officer would act as a deterrent, but he knew that it wouldn't, not if the men attacking were from one of the cartels.

He had called the Stark Police Department and the person that answered assured him that the deputy on site was one of their best and that Sheriff McKay would be given his message as soon as he called in.

Tanner pounded the dashboard and cursed the incompetence of small-town law enforcement. Then he cursed the car for not moving faster, even as the logical part of his brain was telling him that nothing was wrong, and that the odds of Martillo attacking the ranch at that very moment were slim.

But Tanner knew, he knew, and he only hoped that he could make it in time. He thought of Cody, whispered, "Hang on, kid," and drove down the highway like a madman.

∼

WHILE SEATED TOGETHER AT THE KITCHEN TABLE, THE Parkers had just finished eating a late dessert of apple pie when the first shot broke one of the living room windows and shattered the glass front on the grandfather clock, a clock that had been handmade by Frank's late father.

The shot was the first, but the next seventeen that followed were separated by less than a second of time.

Frank Parker had startled at the sound of breaking glass, but as the barrage continued, Cody knew the sound for what it was. He yelled, "Everybody get down!" and then he dived beneath the table, to reach across and pull his sisters from their seats and onto the floor.

The next ten seconds were chaos. Hundreds of rounds entered the house and did to it what a similar attack had done to the McKay home.

Claire was the first to die. A bullet struck her in the head as she was reaching down to free the baby from his high chair. Cody caught her before the body could hit the floor, as his father grabbed the baby.

Frank let out a wail of grief and Cody told him to guard the kids, as he sprinted for his rifle, which he kept in a rack on the rear porch.

"No Cody, stay down!" Frank yelled, but it was too late. The headstrong boy had ahold of his rifle and was headed out the back door.

∼

Cody shot two men, rolled, and shot two more, while a round cut across his left arm. He hadn't felt the wound, hadn't felt anything, except the urge to kill everyone who threatened his family.

At the rear of the home was a decorative metal trellis. Cody climbed up it as if possessed of wings, with the rifle strapped to his back and spare shells jingling in his pockets.

He made it onto the roof of the wraparound porch, and three more men died in the front yard. The others realized where the shots were coming from, and they sent a barrage of bullets into the corner of the house where Cody had been firing from.

Cody kicked in the glass of his father's bedroom window, climbed inside, and before leaving, he reloaded the rifle and removed his father's .44 Magnum from the bedside table.

The sound of the baby's crying seemed to come from everywhere at once and filled the house, giving speed to Cody's legs, as he flew down the steps to rejoin his family.

The front door was kicked in as Cody reached the foot of the stairs. He used his father's gun to send a .44 slug into the chest of the first man he saw, which caused the man to stumble backwards and knock down the two men behind him.

It gave Cody time to make it into the kitchen. His breath caught in his throat when he saw that the walls had been shredded by gunfire, then his heart nearly stopped as he saw that Claire's body had been joined by that of his sister, Jill. The little girl had taken a shot to the chest and the exit wound left a gaping hole in her back.

"Dad!"

"We're in the dining room!"

Cody went low through the swinging door that separated the two rooms and found his father beneath the table with his sister Jessie, and baby James, who was wailing like a banshee.

Frank took his gun from Cody and wiped away tears with his sleeve.

"How many are there, boy?"

Cody spat the words out. "It's a goddamn army."

"That many?"

"I killed seven or eight of them and it was like I didn't even make a dent."

Jessie hugged her brother tightly as she sobbed in spasms of grief. Cody wrapped an arm around her and kissed the top of her head.

"They got Jill, Cody," Jessie moaned.

"I know, baby, and I'm so sorry, I'm so sorry."

The sound of feet crunching over glass came from both the living room and the kitchen. Frank thrust the baby at his daughter and got in front of her to face toward the living room, as Cody took aim at the doorway to the kitchen.

When the sound of the footsteps ceased, Cody intuitively knew what was about to happen.

"They're going to shoot through the walls, get—"

His words were drowned out by the chaotic sounds of destruction and death.

Cody heard his father cry out, his sister scream in pain, but it was the abrupt silence of his baby brother that sickened him. When he turned his head to the right, he saw the obscene wounds, and although they twitched as their bodies shut down, he knew that all three of them were dead. The black grief nearly made Cody give up, but a scarlet fury fired him up to press on.

He'd been hit in the right leg and the lower back during the barrage, but Cody dragged himself toward the windows, and while cutting himself repeatedly, he crawled through broken glass and debris.

When the guns fell silent for reloading, Cody propped up against the windowsill and flipped over to fall to the ground outside.

Limping, his back on fire, he came across two men bent over near the porch. They were looking at a device of some kind. It was a second firebomb, and they were getting it ready to use. Cody shot them both from behind before falling to one knee, as his wounded leg gave out.

As a man ran out the front door, Cody took aim, but he was shot in the chest by Martillo before he could fire. Cody collapsed onto his back with a groan, as the worst pain he'd ever felt took hold of him, and he realized he was dying.

Martillo walked over, pressed the tip of the silencer against Cody's forehead, and said five words.

"You fought like a king."

An instant later, Martillo pulled the trigger.

~

MARTILLO HAD ARRIVED WITH FORTY MEN AND LEFT WITH eight dead and two wounded.

They had killed over a dozen men, destroyed a family, and slaughtered a police officer. The repercussions of the attacks would turn the community of Stark, Texas, into little more than a ghost town for over a decade, and scar both the town and the county forever.

And for a young man calling himself Tanner, it would be a turning point, and the greatest failure of his life.

31

COMING CLEAN ABOUT BEING DIRTY

Tanner had called ahead and told Doc to go to the kitchen and stay there, and that if Javier entered the room, he was to watch him like a hawk.

On his way home, Tanner bought new clothes, ones free of microscopic particles of biker blood and gunshot residue. He changed into them in the dressing room, before discarding his other clothes with the plastic garbage bags he had sat on as he drove the truck.

When he did return to the ranch, he found Javier seated on the porch steps and looking deep in thought. Were it not for the fact that he was Maria's son, Tanner would have wasted him with the rest of the Diablo Boys and ended the threat cleanly.

He approached Javier with a scowl and held out his hand. "Give it to me."

Javier had been so lost in thought, that he hadn't realized Tanner was there.

"What?"

"I said, give it to me."

Javier's bronze face turned almost white, and he licked

his lips several times. "I don't know what you're talking about, Tanner. Now get away from me."

Tanner leaned over and spoke softly. "If you don't give me that bottle, I will make you eat it."

Javier opened his mouth, closed it, opened it again, and then reached into his pocket and removed the bottle. As he was laying it into Tanner's palm, he began sobbing.

"I couldn't do it. Not that, I just couldn't do it."

Javier pointed at the plants beside the porch and Tanner saw the yellowish powder that was laying in the dirt. He then looked inside the bottle and saw that it was empty.

"What were you supposed to do with this?"

"They wanted me to put it in my mother's wine. Jefe' said that it would be like she went to sleep and never woke up."

"What was in this bottle?"

"I don't know, but it came from a bigger bottle that will be planted in Chuck Willis's office. One of the gang, Georgio, he has a cousin that works on the night cleaning crew at Willis's company. She was going to plant the evidence and then call in an anonymous tip."

"So, Willis had nothing to do with this?"

"No, but how did you find out about the Diablo Boys?"

"Never mind that. You need to talk to your mother. If you don't, I will. She needs to know what a piece of shit you are."

Javier straightened his back at that, but then slumped his shoulders in resignation of Tanner's insult, and the truth it contained. A moment later, he reached out and grabbed Tanner by the arm.

"The Diablo Boys will come here when they find out that I couldn't do it. They'll come here and try to kill my mother. You have to do something."

"Don't worry about it; I'll handle it."

Javier covered his face with his hands, as he began crying again. "Oh God, I fucked up. I fucked up so bad."

"What's going on here?"

It was Maria. She had just opened the front door and froze when she saw Javier crying. She came down the porch steps with concern lighting her face.

"What's wrong? Were you two fighting again?"

"No," Tanner said. "But Javier has something to tell you."

~

JAVIER TALKED TO HIS MOTHER IN THE LIVING ROOM WITH Tanner watching, and Tanner was surprised when the boy didn't attempt to sugarcoat anything.

He had begun hanging around the gang six months earlier. They used him as a gofer to fetch coffee and food, as they hung around their makeshift clubhouse at the old Taco Queen.

The Diablo Boys made mule runs or acted as security for a San Antonio drug lord whenever they were needed, which was seldom. However, the mule runs made them more in a day of transporting drugs than most people made in a month. Javier rode along with them once, and that was when Jefe' learned about the ranch.

"He kept asking me if the ranch would be mine someday. I said yeah, that I guessed that you would leave it to me and Romina." Javier paused and looked at his mother with a sad expression. "A week later, Jefe' started saying how nice it would be if you were out of the way, and that with Romina being underage, I would inherit the ranch alone, or at least be in control of it. He had given it a lot of thought and wanted to place an airstrip on the ranch, so that drug planes could land here and turn it into a distribution center. He wanted you out of the way, and he was going to make it happen one way or another."

Maria stood and walked about the room for a moment before she came to stand before Javier.

"Why didn't you go to the police?"

"Jefe' said that if I told anyone it would just be my word against theirs, and that someday soon, Romina would be killed."

"They wanted you to choose between the two of us?" Maria said.

"Not really, they wanted you dead, but they said that if they weren't tied to it, that they would let Romina live."

"And all these 'accidents,' they were all caused by you, even the knife that nearly killed Mrs. Salgado?"

Javier stood and took his mother's hands. "I swear to God I thought that it would just fall out and frighten her, but I guess it flipped when it fell, and the blade end hit her first."

Maria looked stricken. She freed her hands from Javier and settled back on the sofa. After nearly a minute passed, she wiped tears away and spoke to her son, as disappointment showed in her eyes.

"You're going to the police and tell them everything."

"But Mom, they'll hurt Romina, they will."

Tanner spoke up. "No, they won't. I'll make sure of it, but your mother is right. You need to go to the police, and you need to do it as soon as possible."

～

JAVIER AND MARIA SPOKE TO THE COPS. THE NEXT THING Javier knew, he was a suspect in the murders of the Diablo Boys.

Before leaving the gang's clubhouse, Tanner had used Jefe"s phone to dial 9-1-1, before placing the phone back in the gang leader's hand. After tracing the call, the police dispatched a patrol car to the Taco Queen, found the bodies, and the time of Jefe"s death was fixed as occurring after the call was made.

Traffic cameras confirmed that Javier was miles away at the time and a Paraffin test gave the result that his hands were clean of gunshot residue. Also, no trace of blood was found on his clothing. He was back at the ranch with his mother that night, and he no longer had to fear the Diablo Boys Biker Gang.

~

JAVIER JOINED TANNER ON THE PORCH AROUND MIDNIGHT and sat across from him at the card table.

"How did you learn what was going on?"

"Does it matter?" Tanner said.

Javier was silent for several moments before asking the question that was on his mind.

"You killed them, didn't you? Jefe' and the others, it was you?"

"Goodnight, Javier."

Javier walked back to the door, but before he closed it behind him, two words left his lips.

"Thank you."

Tanner rose from his seat to patrol one last time before settling down for a full night's sleep.

32
THE GIFT

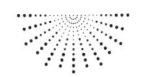

THE PARKER RANCH, SEPTEMBER 1997, TWO DAYS AFTER THE MASSACRE

AT DAWN, TANNER PUSHED ASIDE THE YELLOW POLICE TAPE and walked down the driveway that once led to the home of the Parker family.

Where a home had stood, there was just a foundation and the remains of a crumbled red brick chimney. The blaze that destroyed the structure was so intense that some of the bricks had melted.

He had been too late.

Too late to save them.

And so what?

He was a killer, wasn't he? Not a bodyguard, not a cop, not a savior, but a taker of lives. He would have been truer to himself had he agreed to do the job in the first place, marched over, and massacred the Parker family himself.

It would have been simpler.

It would have been cleaner.

And he wouldn't have the faces of the dead haunting his dreams as they did now, because they would have been strangers. The faces of the twins, Jill and Jessie; of the woman, Claire; of Frank; and even the baby, the goddamn baby that the bastard calling himself Martillo felt it necessary to kill.

"I let you down, Cody," Tanner whispered, and then he thought about his mentor and wondered what the old man would think of this mess.

The name Tanner had been passed down from one assassin to another for nearly a hundred years, but Tanner's mentor, the fifth Tanner, had held the name the longest, and had given him the honor of bearing it when the old man believed he was dying.

"But I'm too young," he had said.

The old man smiled at him and grabbed his hand. "You're the one, boy, because you've got the gift, that rare combination."

"What gift?"

"You're smart and you're deadly, both are needed, but you've got something else. Despite the ice in your veins, there's also a fire deep in your heart. I've known some stone-cold killers who thought they were the baddest thing going, but they were nothing more than killing machines. To be the best, to be a Tanner, that takes heart."

"But we kill people for a living, how much heart does that take?"

The old man smiled again, even as his eyes began to close from exhaustion, exhaustion caused by the disease that was killing him.

"There will come a day when you'll either have to follow your heart or your head, and you'll choose your heart and risk everything for a cause. Not money, but a cause, a just cause. Mere killers run from insurmountable odds, but Tanners, we overcome them."

"Because we're the best?"

"No, because we have heart, and where others run from a fight, we win. That makes us the best."

Tanner left the Parker Ranch and headed for Mexico.

It was time for Martillo to die.

33

MATCHMAKER, MATCHMAKER

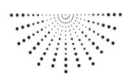

With the ranch safe once more, Tanner no longer had to babysit Romina, who was now riding to and from school with her boyfriend, Chaz Willis. With it being a Saturday, the two kids were off somewhere with friends.

Tanner was planning to leave the ranch soon but stayed on a few days longer to regain his strength after being shot. Doc had removed his stitches the night before and declared that the bullet wound was healing nicely.

Things seemed settled at the ranch, so Tanner was surprised when, while out on a run, he spotted Chuck Willis parked on the side of the road. The man was staring out at a meadow on the Reyes property, where Maria was riding her horse. His car window was down, and when Willis raised his hands and took aim, Tanner ran toward him while reaching for the gun at the small of his back.

However, when he got a good look at what Willis was holding, he relaxed, then shook his head in dismay.

"Just ask the woman out already," Tanner said. His sudden appearance startled Willis so much that he dropped the camera he was holding.

"Mr. Tanner, um, hello."

"Do you spy on women often, Willis?"

"No, but I saw her riding and I… Hell, Tanner, I like the woman, and she's so beautiful I can barely speak when I'm around her."

"You're giving me a lift back to the ranch, then you and Maria are going to talk."

Willis gave him a pained expression. "The woman hates me."

Tanner opened the passenger door. "She doesn't hate you, and anyway, there's something she needs to say to you. Now get moving. I want to be there when she returns from her ride."

∽

Doc took the horse's reins from Maria as she dismounted, then she walked toward Chuck Willis with her hand extended.

"Mr. Willis, welcome to my ranch."

Willis appeared startled by her civil greeting. When he took her hand, Maria held his hand in both of hers and offered an apology for the way she acted at their last meeting.

Tanner suggested that they move things inside, and soon they were having coffee in the living room.

∽

"A biker gang?" Willis said.

"Yes and… I'm sad to have to admit it, but my son was responsible for most of what went on, the things I blamed you for, and again, I apologize."

"Willis has a new offer for you, Maria," Tanner said.

Maria's demeanor grew colder, as she stared at Willis. "I won't sell at any price."

"Tell her, Willis," Tanner said.

"Oh, yes, I no longer want to buy your land, but I would like to lease its use for one month every year, not all of it, just the southern pasture."

"Why would you want to do that?"

"I'm building on the last of my land, the property that used to be the McKay Ranch, but for the past several years I've let the town use it each October for the Fall Fair. I was hoping that you'd be kind enough to let me lease your land, so that the fair can be held here instead."

Maria looked thoughtful for a moment before speaking.

"No, I won't lease it to you, but I will let the town use it for free. I love the Fall Fair."

Willis smiled. "Excellent, the mayor will be happy with that arrangement. I'll tell her to give you a call."

"Mr. Willis?"

"Please, call me Chuck."

"All right, Chuck, would you like to come by for dinner tonight? Your son will be here, and I think as neighbors that we should get to know each other better."

Willis said nothing for a moment, but then nodded emphatically. "I would love to have dinner with you, Mrs. Reyes."

"Call me, Maria."

Willis smiled. "I'll do that, Maria."

Tanner stood. "I'll leave you two to talk."

He entered the hallway and found Javier walking toward him. "What's up, Javier?"

The kid shrugged. While at the police station, and at Maria's insistence, he had confessed to staging the accidents around the ranch.

Luckily for him, none of the employees who had been hurt were pressing charges, but he still faced a charge of criminal mischief.

"My lawyer thinks I'll be sentenced to three months of community service."

"I'll be sure to litter the next time I drive on the highway, so you'll have something to pick up."

"Funny, Tanner. I'll also be going to school in the fall. Mom said it was either that or join the army."

"A free college education? Things could be worse."

"Yeah."

Javier went into the kitchen, while Tanner headed to the apartment above the barn, where he showered and changed into jeans and a plain white T-shirt.

Afterwards, he settled down to read, but found himself too restless to concentrate. He left the apartment with a sigh, to begin walking toward the graves of the Parker family.

34
"I'M DEATH!"

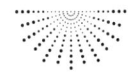

MATAMOROS, MEXICO, OCTOBER 1997

Tanner had been in Mexico for over three weeks when he decided to make his move on Martillo.

He had originally planned to kill Martillo at the bar the man owned and frequented on Avenida Marte R. Gómez. He decided against it, after learning through surveillance that the cops Martillo had on the take worked out of a building a block away from the bar.

That meant he might have to face armed police officers when he made his escape, and the odds could be over a dozen to one and turn him into a cop killer.

Tanner wanted it to be cleaner than that, so he decided to hit Martillo at his villa, which was well guarded, but also secluded. The two-story home was beautiful, with a large pool, well-tended garden, and a six-car garage. It was where Martillo kept his collection of classic cars, including a 1931 Rolls Royce Phantom.

There was a cobblestone path that circumnavigated the

home, with adjacent paths that led to the gate, the garage, and a small structure that housed a backup generator.

The villa sat at the top of a hill that was accessible by one long winding road and the view from the gate shack looked out over it. Any car coming up would be seen from miles away and the trip along the steep switchback road took minutes to complete.

The rear of the compound faced a mile of dense vegetation with thorny plants, followed by a nearly perpendicular drop down to a rock-strewn river.

The home was surrounded by a wall on all sides, but the security was flawed, because the trees at the rear of the property had been allowed to grow too tall, and their branches hung above the walls. That was where Tanner perched himself and did surveillance, after climbing up from the river and traversing the prickly field.

By the fifth time he'd made the trip back and forth, and up and down to the villa, he had the route and its intricacies mapped out in his mind and could climb the cliff and navigate through the field quickly. That would be a huge advantage when it came time to escape, that is, if he lived through the attack.

He spent weeks watching the place off and on, marking down the number of guards, their shifts and the times they patrolled.

Martillo had at least ten men with him almost all the time, but only two of them, his lieutenants, or as he referred to them, his Caballeros, or Knights, lived on the property with him. They had their own rooms, which were the size of many apartments.

The Knights' schedules predominantly mirrored that of Martillo's, but one of the men had a woman that he visited in a neighboring town once a week, during her husband's weekly card game.

His absence meant that, not counting Martillo, there would be nine men to deal with instead of ten when he was gone.

That took place on Saturday night, which was also the night that Martillo would indulge himself with a whore or two, despite being a married man. And while their leader was otherwise occupied, the guards seemed much more lax while performing their duties. Tanner had even seen the gate guard leave his post so that he could bullshit with the other men in the villa.

That left only one of Martillo's Knights roaming about the home on Saturday night. As far as Tanner could tell, the man did nothing but work on what looked like a computer, as he could see the reflection of the screen's glow on the lens of the man's glasses.

He surmised that the man handled Martillo's records and money, while the other Knight oversaw distribution. If so, it was no wonder he kept them close to him.

With Saturday night deemed to be the best time to strike, Tanner waited patiently for the next one to arrive. When it came, he slipped over the villa's outer wall like a ghost dressed in black.

He carried a MAC-10 that had belonged to his mentor, the fifth Tanner. It had a two-stage suppressor, shot .45 ACP rounds and was as deadly as the Heckler & Koch MP5s that Martillo's men had used to slaughter the Parkers and McKay.

Tanner killed his first man with a silent blast, as the guard rounded the corner of the home. The man's eyes widened in surprise, but only after the bullets struck, as he had failed to notice Tanner hiding in the shadows.

Because the guards patrolled the grounds in a crisscrossing fashion, Tanner knew he had to kill the guard coming from the other direction. Thanks to his surveillance, he knew that the man would reach his position in just over a minute.

Tanner used some of that time to drag the first man's body off the cobblestone path, then moved back into the shadows to wait once more.

The second sentry arrived forty-three seconds later, but they felt closer to forty-three minutes to Tanner. He sent another blast from his gun at the guard as he walked nearer to his position. Two of the bullets hit the man in the chest, near his heart, while the third round passed beneath his armpit and shattered a window behind him.

The noise of the falling glass sounded like thunder and Tanner knew that the time for stealth had ended, because a light came on in a window.

The guard who filled in at night after the housekeeper left looked outside, saw the body on the path, and screamed out that there was an intruder. Tanner sent six shots at the window and the man's shouts of alarm ceased.

Not counting Martillo and his knight there were still five guards left and a call would go out for more to rush to the villa. Tanner knew from watching the place that this meant he had ten minutes at best before reinforcements showed. A good portion of that time would be spent by the men driving up the winding hill and opening the gates.

Tanner left the shadows, strode across the path, and shot the lock on a side door to pieces. He would enter Martillo's home the way Martillo invaded the Parker ranch, and he wouldn't stop killing until either he or Martillo was dead.

~

One more guard died without even knowing it, as Tanner shot the man in the head from behind the door the man had just opened.

The sound of the body hitting the floor was louder than the shot Tanner had fired. Still, he doubted that the killing had been overheard.

Up the stairs a door opened, followed by the appearance of Martillo's Knight accountant. He was a man of about forty with the trim, long-muscled build of a swimmer. He was wearing rimless glasses that made his eyes look huge.

The fool had his arms full as he carried his computer, and he nearly tripped on the cord as he was rushing down the stairs.

It wasn't until he reached the landing that he noticed the body. After gasping in surprise, he spotted Tanner and froze like a statue, with only his eyes moving in frantic patterns behind the eyeglasses.

Footsteps came from beyond the open front doorway and a man called out the first guard's name, as he spotted the body lying inside.

After entering, the man looked up at the frozen accountant, so Tanner used the distraction to cut him down with six shots before reloading.

The fool with the computer made for great bait. Tanner wouldn't have minded if he stayed there longer, but the man let out a yell and tried to go back up the flight of stairs he'd come down.

Tanner's gloved hand held the gun's long silencer like a foregrip, as he aimed upward and sent three rounds at the accountant. They passed through the computer and sent the man sliding to the floor, where his face lay buried in a corner of the landing. That left Martillo and three guards to go, as the clock ticked away, and reinforcements converged.

Tanner headed up the steps, past the captured Knight, and was running up the second flight of stairs when a spray of gunfire nearly cut him down. The three remaining guards had appeared and were chasing after him.

The hallway of the second floor was wide enough to drive a car down, and there were several doors on either side. A pair of ornate doors were at the hallway's end. They led into Martillo's bedroom.

Tanner kicked open one of the doors on his left, entered the dark room in a crouch, and lay on the floor in the shadows just beyond the reach of the light spilling in from the hallway.

The guards followed behind, and within seconds, they were gathered outside the doorway. Tanner shielded his gun with his body to avoid any muzzle flash being seen and fired one shot toward the three windows the room had. He was hoping to make the guards think he was attempting to escape that way.

It worked. Two of the guards filled the doorway with guns blazing at chest level toward the opposite wall, where the windows were.

Tanner fired upwards from his position on the floor and the two men grunted and fell backwards, and before the other guard could catch his bearings, Tanner stood and charged the hallway. He and the guard exchanged two shots before hitting each other.

Tanner's shot had ripped through the man's throat, while the guard's shot had caught him on the right side, just below the Kevlar vest he wore. Tanner could feel the warm blood leaking onto his hip as he fell to his knees.

He moaned, as the pain was intense, but the shot had

only dug a groove in his flesh and had caused no real damage. He stood and sent more shots into the men at his feet, because two of them, although gravely wounded, were still moving. After reloading, Tanner went to kill Martillo.

~

As he expected, the man was using the woman with him as a shield.

Martillo stood with a machine pistol in his right hand while his left held the woman by her hair. She was a voluptuous beauty still in her teens and was trembling from fear.

Both Martillo and the woman were naked and facing the double doors that led to the hallway. Martillo had no idea that Tanner was behind them on the balcony.

After killing the last of the guards, Tanner had climbed out the shattered windows of the room he'd just left. He then inched along the stone border that encircled the home, and which had decorative patterns carved upon its face.

It took him more than two valuable minutes to traverse the thirty feet that separated the room from the balcony, but the stone shelf he inched along was only six inches wide. A misstep would have resulted in a fall, and possibly broken bones, to be followed by death.

Martillo had given up on shouting for his men and was demanding that someone speak to him, while insisting that an agreement could be reached. He was trying to stall until his fresh troops arrived, but time was something he'd run out of.

Tanner sent an angled shot through the patio doors that struck Martillo in the flesh of his left buttock. The man released the hooker and instinctively felt for the wound.

"Drop the gun or die," Tanner said in Spanish, and Martillo turned and looked at him with hope in his eyes.

"I'll drop it, see?" Martillo said, then he tossed the gun onto the bed.

Tanner shouted for the girl to leave. She gathered up her clothes and fumbled at the locked door while whimpering. Once she had it open, she ran off as fast as she could, down the hall, and past the bodies of the dead guards.

Martillo limped over to lean on the footboard, while gesturing with his head at the fleeing girl.

"That was some good tail; you should have taken a turn."

Martillo's mood was light, because he took from the fact that he was still alive that he was going to remain so, but the assumption was false. Tanner's plans for him did not include his staying alive, but of dying a fitting death.

A glint above the headboard caught Tanner's eye. He made a huffing sound as he realized what he was looking at.

It was a gold-plated hammer with the word Martillo, engraved upon its face in cursive script. It wasn't a claw hammer, such as the type commonly used, but more like a two-pound sledge with a foot-long handle. Tanner sent a blast from the gun in its direction and shattered the glass case it sat in.

Martillo watched Tanner examine the hammer. "You like that, eh?"

"I do," Tanner said. "Now, let's see how you like it."

He charged at Martillo and smashed the hammer across his face. And before the drug lord could spit out his broken teeth, Tanner went to work on the man's kneecaps.

By the time Tanner had finished, Martillo had two broken knees and elbows to match. The bones were more than broken, they had been crushed.

The Hammer had been hammered, and judging by the moans coming from him, he had not enjoyed it.

Tanner got down on one knee and spoke to Martillo. "I left you alive so that you could enjoy the rest of the show. I'm going to burn this place down around you."

Martillo gazed up at Tanner with eyes full of hate, as he mumbled out words past bloody jagged stumps that used to be teeth, set in a jaw that canted to the left.

"Who… are… you?"

"I'm death!" Tanner said, and then he rushed from the room as Martillo struggled in vain to stand, or even crawl.

∞

TANNER ROCKETED DOWN THE STAIRS. IT WASN'T UNTIL HE reached the bottom that he realized the body of the accountant wasn't on the landing.

He went back up and saw that the damaged computer was sitting in a puddle of blood, but that the man himself had escaped.

There was no time to search for him and he was of little consequence, so Tanner went about applying the finishing touches.

Before gathering the materials he needed, he took in the view of the twisting road that led to the villa. He saw the headlights of three cars. Two of the cars were at the bottom and still a few minutes away, while the first one was farther along and would arrive sooner. Its occupants still had to deal with rolling back the locked gates and gaining entrance.

Tanner was intending to head toward a shed on the

side of the house, where he knew the groundskeeper kept gasoline for the lawnmower, but as soon as he stepped out onto the patio, he saw something just as good by the red brick grill.

A minute later, he had squirted a liter of lighter fluid throughout the house and up the stairs. After setting a rolled newspaper on fire, he heard the squeal of brakes, followed by the sound of car doors opening and closing outside.

He waited until the first of the fresh guards stepped through the doorway. When a man appeared holding an assault rifle, Tanner dropped the flaming newspaper, which set the home ablaze and drove the man back outside with his pant leg on fire.

Tanner ran back to the bedroom where Martillo still lay moaning on the floor. He then emptied the last few drops of the lighter fluid onto the bed and set it aflame.

"Burn in hell, Martillo!"

Martillo wasn't listening; his gaze was concentrated upon the flaming bed and the smoke filling the room.

Tanner turned his back on him, sprinted onto the balcony, and leapt out into the night to fall into the pool below. When he surfaced from beneath the water, he found the air thick with smoke, as flames lit the villa with an eerie glow.

Tanner made it to the back wall, scrambled over it with some difficulty, thanks to the wound on his side, and disappeared into the night, only pausing once to look back at the glow of flames caused by his handiwork.

He whispered, "That was for you, Cody," and then he faded like a shadow at dawn.

35
"SAY MY NAME."

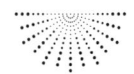

At the Reyes Ranch, Tonya joined Tanner at the small cemetery that held the remains of the Parkers.

Tonya was wearing a blue dress. Her tanned legs were shapely, while just a touch of cleavage showed up top.

"I come here at least once a year, usually on the twins' birthday. I still miss Jill and Jessie very much."

Tanner turned and looked at her, saw in her eyes that she knew, that she'd remembered. He felt the strange sense of relief that the kinship of that knowledge gave him.

"You three were more like sisters than friends," he said.

Tonya took his hand. "I remembered you the first time I saw you, but it had been a lot of years and, for obvious reasons, my mind rejected the feelings and thoughts I had. I spent the last few days trying to recall the name of the man who had been staying here at the time of the murders, and I finally did last night. His name was Tanner."

"Yes."

Tonya pointed down at the grave before them, the

grave of Cody Parker, then she turned and took his face in her hands.

"How is it possible you're standing here?"

"It was Tanner, the other Tanner, he saved me."

"And you're really, you're…"

"Say it."

"You're Cody Parker."

Tanner nodded.

"Yes, I'm Cody Parker."

36

APPRENTICE

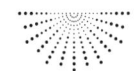

THE PARKER RANCH, STARK, TEXAS, SEPTEMBER 1997

CODY WAS SHOT IN THE CHEST BY MARTILLO BEFORE HE could fire again. As he collapsed onto his back with a groan, he realized he was dying.

Martillo walked over, pressed the tip of the silencer against Cody's forehead, and said five words.

"You fought like a king."

An instant later, Martillo pulled the trigger, but the shot went into the dirt beside Cody's head, as Martillo was tackled to the ground by the boy, Pablo.

The Mexican teen was crying and screaming in outrage as he clawed at Martillo's throat. He had lied to the Parkers when he told them that his parents had been killed while on his father's fishing boat. His father hadn't been a fisherman, but a farmer. When his father refused to grow poppies for the local drug lord instead of the food the village desperately needed to survive, the man had him, and his entire family murdered by men much like the ones who were killing the Parkers. Only Pablo escaped the slaughter, and seeing it happen again had driven him mad with rage.

A single shot could be heard, partly muffled by a failing sound suppressor, but clearly audible. Pablo arched his back with a face set in a rictus of pain, before sliding off Martillo to lay in the dirt.

Martillo rose in a fury and emptied the rest of his weapon into the dying boy, reloaded, and then emptied it again, before kicking what was left of the body.

Afterward, Martillo turned from Pablo's mutilated corpse and shouted for his men to set the timer on the bomb. As he spoke, he ran a hand over his thick throat and felt the bloody gouges left there by Pablo's hands.

"Vámonos!"

Martillo and his men dragged off their dead and wounded confederates, while leaving behind a nightmare of death, and yet, there was one survivor amid the massacre.

A boy named Cody Parker, mortally wounded, and too weakened by his wounds to move, yet alive, alive.

∽

TANNER NEARLY RAN HEAD-ON INTO THE DEPARTING tractor-trailer as he made the final turn before reaching the Parker Ranch.

He skidded onto the shoulder, trampled sagebrush with his rear tires, and drove past the bullet-riddled police car with the dead deputy inside. He reached the other end of the driveway just as the bomb exploded and set the home ablaze.

"No!"

After leaving the highway, he had seen the glow of the fire at the McKay Ranch and knew that he had been right, and that Martillo was on the hunt for revenge that night.

Tanner skidded the car to a stop beside the porch, saw the savage flames emerging through the front door, and realized that anyone inside the house was gone.

He then turned and looked out at the yard, where over a thousand shell casings glistened in the firelight, and he knew that Martillo had truly sent an army to the ranch.

That's when he spotted Cody lying in the dirt.

Tanner moved the car beside him, stepped out of it, and felt as if he were inside a blast furnace, as hot air, smoke, and ash swirled about him.

He almost tripped over Pablo on his way to Cody and saw what over four dozen rounds could do to a body. Pablo's head was a bloody pulp with limbs shredded by multiple close-range wounds.

"Cody?"

When there was no response, Tanner thought the boy to be dead, but when he rested a hand on his chest below the vicious wound, he felt movement.

"Hold on, Cody, hold on!"

Tanner lifted Cody and placed him across the rear seat, then sighed in despair at the flaming house. After a second of hesitation, he plucked Cody's old Remington from the ground and placed it beside him.

He had gone barely fifty feet on his way toward the driveway when the explosion occurred, as the flames found the gas line. The blast caused the rear of the home to collapse, while the burning roof of the front porch tumbled into the yard to land on the body of Pablo, crushing what was left of it, while acting as his funeral pyre.

The force of the explosion lifted the driver's side of the

car, but when the wheels touched ground again, Tanner raced out the driveway and away.

A mile later, when he spotted a pay phone in front of a closed gas station, Tanner pulled over and made a call.

"I need to speak to Mr. Mastriani."

"Who's calling?" said a gruff voice.

"Tell him it's Tanner."

Two minutes later, a smooth male voice came on the line. "Tanner, how are you, kid?"

"I need help. I have a wounded bird that needs mending."

"I see, but you do understand that the vet doesn't come cheaply?"

"I do, and the next time there's a mess I'll clean up for free."

A pause, then the voice spoke again. "Two messes, agreed?"

Tanner closed his eyes. The bastard was going to milk him.

"Agreed."

"And one more thing."

"Yes?"

"Carlo's boy, the one who wants to do what you do, do you know the one I mean?"

"I do, but what about him?"

"He tags along on the next clean-up; I believe he's done that once before, no?"

"Yes, I took him along as a favor to Carlo and I'll do it again, but this bird is very fragile, so I'll need the vet right away."

"He'll be waiting for you. You know the place, right?"

"I do, and thank you, Mr. Mastriani."

"My pleasure, Tanner, and good luck with your wounded bird."

Tanner returned to the car and found that Cody was still breathing, yet still unconscious. He drove on, headed toward help, and thought about the Parkers, the ones beyond saving.

He pounded the steering wheel in anger. "I should have been there!"

And he would have died; he knew it. The multitude of shell casings had told the tale of the force arrayed against the home. One more gun would have made little difference.

After glancing into the back seat at the boy he had come to care for, Tanner vowed that he would save him.

∽

CODY AWOKE LATE THE NEXT DAY.

He was in the basement of a bordello where the San Antonio mob kept an illegal clinic. The space was also used on rare occasions to torture, as the room was soundproof.

Cody was still too weak to even sit up, but the doctor, a thoracic surgeon with an out-of-control gambling habit, assured him that he would make a full recovery, but that it would take time.

Tanner sat by his bed, as Cody relayed the details of Martillo's attack, ending with Pablo's brave attempt to save him.

"He did save you," Tanner said. "If not for him, you wouldn't be here."

Tanner held up a newspaper, whose headline declared that the Parker family had been slain, Cody included.

"They think I'm dead?"

"It's Pablo. He's been misidentified as being you. I'm not surprised, between the bullets and the flames, there couldn't have been much left for an autopsy, and it's a logical assumption."

Cody closed his eyes and Tanner thought he had drifted off to sleep, but then the boy spoke.

"If I come forward, they won't let me live, will they?"

"No, the cartel never forgets, and they know you killed several of their men."

"What if when I'm better, what if then I kill this guy Martillo?"

"Then they would want you for that. Cody Parker is on their radar, or he was, but now they think he's dead."

"And I have to stay dead?"

"It's the only way to stay safe."

"I don't want to stay safe. I want revenge."

The heart monitor attached to Cody began to beep loudly. Tanner laid a hand on his shoulder.

"Just get better, that's all you have to do."

"And then what? Contact the cops and enter Witness Protection?"

Tanner shook his head. "If I thought that was safe, you'd be in a real hospital right now. With the reach the cartel has, I figured it was a fifty-fifty chance that you'd be hit before you ever saw a Fed. You're a witness to a massacre, one that already has the country up in arms over illegal immigration and the failure of the drug war. If the cartel didn't kill you, someone in DC might order it done."

Cody wiped at tears. "They're gone, Tanner. Jill, Jessie, my dad, Claire… and the baby, little James, they're all dead… all dead."

When the boy's tears dried, Tanner spoke.

"You're not alone, Cody, you've got me. You know, on the day we found out that Pablo had been hiding in the barn, I told your father that he had done a good thing in taking the boy in and feeding him, giving him a job, a chance. Frank said that he prayed someone would return the favor if one of his children was left all alone. I know I'm not much and I'm hardly a father figure, but I'll look out for you if you'll let me. I think we both know that I owe you at least that much."

"You don't owe me a thing, Tanner. If you had been there, nothing would have changed, there were just too many of them."

"Still, what do you say to my offer?"

"Yes, but I want to learn to do what you do. I want to become the best there is at killing, and then someday it won't matter how many they send, because I'll just kill them all."

"It's a tough life, a lonely life."

Eyes that had been filled with tears turned to stone before Tanner's gaze, and he realized that the tough boy's soul had just hardened a little more.

"I've got nothing left, and any life I live will be less than the one I lost."

"True," Tanner said.

He stayed with Cody until the boy drifted off to sleep, and after leaving him a note, he left to prepare for his trip to Mexico to kill Martillo.

37
IT'S GOOD TO BE HOME

Tonya gazed down at the grave of Cody Parker.

"Pablo is in your grave?"

"Yes, and a few weeks later, Tanner and I left the area."

"And you took his name, and now you do what he did, you guard people?"

Knowing that the truth would only upset Tonya and spawn more questions, Tanner just nodded his head in answer.

"I see, but why take his name?"

"It's a tradition, one passed down from mentor to apprentice. He was the sixth Tanner and I'm the seventh."

"Would the cartel still harm you after all this time?"

"I'm not sure, but I've also no reason to step forward."

"Why did you come back now?"

"Circumstances placed me in the area and curiosity brought me back here. When I learned that there was trouble again, I stayed."

"You were afraid history would repeat itself, weren't you?"

"I was going to make certain the Reyes family stayed safe."

"Which they are thanks to you. Does that mean you'll be leaving soon?"

"I leave tomorrow morning."

"So soon?"

"I have business in New York City that I need to see to, a certain debt to repay."

"And will you ever come back?"

Tanner opened his mouth to say no, but he equivocated instead.

"Who's to say?"

~

They left the graveyard and were walking across a sunlit meadow toward the house when Tonya stopped and grabbed Tanner by the arm.

"The wound to your chest… can I see it?"

Tanner removed his T-shirt and Tonya studied the scar, then she noticed the fresh one below his left collarbone.

"This one looks new, was it as bad as the other one?"

"No."

She moved closer. "Let me kiss it and make it better."

Her lips brushed against the scar, then moved up to find his. Within seconds, they were lying on the grass and kissing passionately. Tanner slipped a hand beneath the dress and soon Tonya was moaning with pleasure, as her own hands went to work on his jeans.

They made love in the meadow, upon the land his family once owned, in the place where he was born and where he was believed to have died.

Tonya the woman was fulfilling a fantasy that Tonya the girl could have scarcely imagined, as the boy of her dreams, Cody Parker, made love to her. She wanted nothing more from him than to have this memory, and to take joy from the fact that he was alive.

"Ooohh, Cody."

Tonya was straddling him, riding him. Tanner reached up and caressed her cheek.

"Call me Tanner."

"Yes," she whispered. "Our little secret."

Tanner smiled. "But not the only one."

"Trey can have me forever. But right now, I'm all yours."

"Tonya."

"Yes?"

Tanner ran his hands over her breasts.

"It's good to be home."

Tonya laughed, and it was followed by a whoop of joy, as Tanner flipped her onto her back, and the two of them became reacquainted.

38

LOST AND FOUND

Romina hugged Tanner so tightly that the ribs he thought were fully healed began to ache again. He reciprocated and embraced her with genuine affection. They were outside the ranch house with Maria, Javier, and Doc, as Tanner prepared to leave in a rented car.

Romina wiped at tears. "I'm going to miss you, Tanner."

"I'll miss you too, and remember what I said."

"I will."

Earlier, Tanner had given Romina a slip of paper with a phone number on it, along with a P.O. Box number. He'd told her that she was to call or write if she ever needed to contact him.

"A man named Tim will answer, or else leave a message and Tim will contact me. Now, that number doesn't have to be used only for emergencies, but I also don't want to gossip about the latest boy band."

Romina had looked down at the paper in her hand. "Who else has this number?"

"Only you."

That made her grin, and she gave Tanner a peck on the lips.

She kissed him once more now, as tears fell from her eyes, and Tanner felt something for her that he had only felt for his sisters and believed he would never feel again. It was a familial protectiveness. Despite the strangeness of it after so many years of absence, he liked the feeling.

Maria hugged him as she thanked him, and she told him he would always be welcome in her home.

"That means more than you know, Maria, thank you."

Javier stepped forward with an offered hand. Tanner shook it while locking eyes with him.

"You don't have to worry about me, dude. I'll be cool."

"Or else," Tanner said. Javier swallowed hard, released his hand, and took a step backwards, as Doc moved forward and pointed at the car.

"You're leaving in better style than when you arrived."

"You're also doing better; and you've found that place to settle down that you were looking for."

"That I did, but what about you, are you ever going to find a home?"

Tanner looked at the Reyes' house, which occupied the very spot of the home he grew up in. For just a moment, he could see it again, along with the people who had lived within it, including his long-dead mother.

"For now, I'm sustained by memories."

A minute later and he was driving away with a sense of something lost, as well as a feeling of something gained, perhaps even reclaimed.

39
SHADES OF THE FUTURE

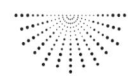

THE PARKER RANCH, STARK, TEXAS, NOVEMBER 1997

A FEW DAYS EARLIER, ON WHAT WOULD HAVE BEEN HIS seventeenth birthday, Cody Parker had been given documents that gave him a new identity and raised his age to nineteen.

He was now Xavier Zane. It was the first of many false identities he would use over the years, and the one he would be known by as he pursued his apprenticeship with Tanner.

He and Tanner stepped out of the car, the one taken from Jack Sheer, and both stood before the rubble that was all that remained of his home.

There were dead flowers everywhere, along with teddy bears left as remembrance for baby James. The community had held a memorial service for the Parkers weeks earlier, but now the wilted petals drifted in the breeze like withered memories. The teddy bears, once bright with color, were faded from exposure to the sun, and streaked with sand and grime.

Cody stood there in the light of a new day as he thought about all he had lost. Taking his cue from the boy, Tanner remained silent as well. After several minutes passed, Cody wiped at his eyes, then turned to Tanner.

"I'm ready to go."

They picked up their bags and walked past Sheer's car, abandoning it, as they would be using another vehicle, which was to be delivered to them by a young man.

It was part of the deal Tanner had made with Mr. Mastriani, to let someone tag along to see how he worked. So, Tanner temporarily had two apprentices. As he walked out to the road, he saw that the other one had arrived on time. That was a good sign.

What was also a good sign was that the kid had moved into the back seat after parking the car, knowing that Tanner would want to take the wheel.

One of Mr. Mastriani's men in Dallas was skimming off the take. Tanner was going to make sure that it stopped, permanently.

After stowing their bags in the trunk, Tanner introduced the two teens.

"Xavier, say hello to Romeo."

Cody looked into the back seat and saw a boy who was about his age. He had spiked blond hair, mirrored sunglasses, and several tattoos on each arm. When the boy spoke, he sounded as if he had been raised in Malibu rather than Dallas.

"Hi, Romeo," Cody said.

"Hey dude, I'm glad you're coming along, because Tanner is boring as shit, but he sure can shoot."

"That he can," Cody said, as he climbed into the passenger seat.

As they began the drive, Tanner loaded a CD. The compact disc didn't hold music, but rather a language course to learn German.

Romeo groaned. "Oh, not that shit again. Hey Xavier, do you believe this dude? And those CDs work too, Tanner speaks like three languages or something."

"Four," Tanner said. "And it wouldn't hurt you to learn something."

"Screw that, I got my Walkman and I'm gonna listen to some tunes."

Cody looked into the back seat and saw Romeo with the headphones on. He was bopping in place to a tune that only he could hear.

The language disc seemed interesting, so Cody turned it up a little.

"Do you really speak four languages?"

Tanner nodded. "I sure do, and it comes in handy sometimes."

They drove along with the CD playing, as they both repeated the new language they were learning. Once the CD played through, Tanner shut it off and the car grew quiet, as Romeo had fallen asleep in the back.

"Tanner."

"Yeah?"

"Thank you. Without you... I don't know what I'd do."

"You'll make it, Cody; you're as tough as they come."

And as the town of Stark, Texas fell farther and farther behind him, Cody Parker headed toward his future.

40

RABID BITCH

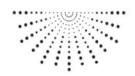

After scouting out the area on foot and watching the house for hours, Tanner felt it safe to drive onto the property.

He was back at the farm in Ridge Creek, Pennsylvania, where he had to check on things and thank someone for helping out.

Edwin "Buck" Seevers opened the door before Tanner could knock, then gestured for him to come inside.

"Tanner, imagine how surprised I was when that guy Tim called and mentioned your name. I thought he was a Vegas cop at first."

"Thanks for coming. I needed someone to play a part and I immediately thought of you."

"No problem, and everything went smoothly. I pretended to be the horrified property owner and now the Feds and the state police have moved on. But keep an eye out for that new police chief, she's a sharp one."

The interior of the farmhouse had been cleaned of all traces of violence, and a new refrigerator sat where the old one had been.

Instead of placing the farm up for sale again, Madison suggested to Tim that he should donate it to a worthy charity, many of which could put the land and home to good use. They were in the process of choosing one.

Tanner spoke to Buck as the actor started his rental.

"Where to now, back to LA?"

Buck made a face of disgust. "I spent years wanting to go there and found out that I hated it. Besides, I'm more of a theater guy. I'm going to New York and try to get a part in an off-Broadway play. And after that, who knows."

"I wish you luck."

A sense of sadness came over Buck and he looked up at Tanner and sighed. "I heard what happened to those kids, Cindy and Billy. It made me sick to my stomach."

Tanner just nodded in agreement.

"There's something you should know, Tanner. I ran into a buddy of mine who left Colorado after O'Grady was killed. He said that O'Grady's daughter is on the warpath to find whoever killed her father. I remember Ariana O'Grady, and that's one mean bitch. Watch your back."

"Why do you assume it was me who killed O'Grady?"

Buck smiled. "I heard it was a professional hit, and for some reason you came to mind."

"If I ever find myself in Colorado again I'll be extra careful, but if O'Grady's daughter wants me dead, she's going to have to get in line."

Buck placed the car in gear. "It's off to fame and fortune I go."

Tanner watched the car drive away, then prepared to leave as well.

In the back of his mind, Tanner wondered if Sara

Blake would still be in Ridge Creek on the off chance that he would return.

∽

When the attack came and she charged at him from the bushes, he was ready. Tanner shot her in the chest twice, and still she almost managed to reach him.

It was the dog, Madison's dog, and it was out of its mind with rabies.

Tanner grimaced as he watched the animal die, although he knew he had only put it out of its misery.

The hound had lost considerable weight during the short time he was gone. He reasoned that the disease must have taken root since the last time he saw her, or perhaps even earlier.

There were still tools in the barn, so he wrapped her in a blanket and buried her near the line of trees at the rear of the farmhouse.

Her tombstone was a simple one since the dog had never had a name. Tanner marked the spot with a cross made from white fence pickets.

With the grim task completed, he walked to his car, left the farm for the last time, and headed for New York City.

There was another rabid bitch that had to be put down, and her name was Sara Blake.

TANNER RETURNS!

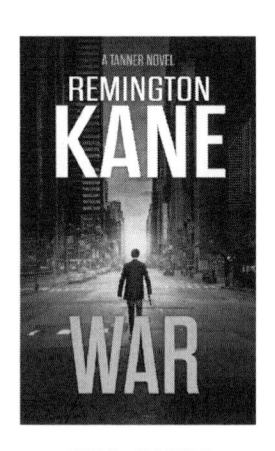

WAR - BOOK 6

AFTERWORD

Thank you,

REMINGTON KANE

JOIN MY INNER CIRCLE

You'll receive FREE books, such as,

SLAY BELLS – A TANNER NOVEL – BOOK 0
    TAKEN! ALPHABET SERIES – 26 ORIGINAL TAKEN! TALES

Also – Exclusive short stories featuring TANNER, along with other books.

TO BECOME AN INNER CIRCLE MEMBER, GO TO:
    http://remingtonkane.com/mailing-list/

ALSO BY REMINGTON KANE

The TANNER Series in order

INEVITABLE I - A Tanner Novel - Book 1

KILL IN PLAIN SIGHT - A Tanner Novel - Book 2

MAKING A KILLING ON WALL STREET - A Tanner Novel - Book 3

THE FIRST ONE TO DIE LOSES - A Tanner Novel - Book 4

THE LIFE & DEATH OF CODY PARKER - A Tanner Novel - Book 5

WAR - A Tanner Novel- A Tanner Novel - Book 6

SUICIDE OR DEATH - A Tanner Novel - Book 7

TWO FOR THE KILL - A Tanner Novel - Book 8

BALLET OF DEATH - A Tanner Novel - Book 9

MORE DANGEROUS THAN MAN - A Tanner Novel - Book 10

TANNER TIMES TWO - A Tanner Novel - Book 11

OCCUPATION: DEATH - A Tanner Novel - Book 12

HELL FOR HIRE - A Tanner Novel - Book 13

A HOME TO DIE FOR - A Tanner Novel - Book 14

FIRE WITH FIRE - A Tanner Novel - Book 15

TO KILL A KILLER - A Tanner Novel - Book 16

WHITE HELL – A Tanner Novel - Book 17

MANHATTAN HIT MAN – A Tanner Novel - Book 18

ONE HUNDRED YEARS OF TANNER – A Tanner Novel -

Book 19

REVELATIONS - A Tanner Novel - Book 20

THE SPY GAME - A Tanner Novel - Book 21

A VICTIM OF CIRCUMSTANCE - A Tanner Novel - Book 22

A MAN OF RESPECT - A Tanner Novel - Book 23

THE MAN, THE MYTH - A Tanner Novel - Book 24

ALL-OUT WAR - A Tanner Novel - Book 25

THE REAL DEAL - A Tanner Novel - Book 26

WAR ZONE - A Tanner Novel - Book 27

ULTIMATE ASSASSIN - A Tanner Novel - Book 28

KNIGHT TIME - A Tanner Novel - Book 29

PROTECTOR - A Tanner Novel - Book 30

BULLETS BEFORE BREAKFAST - A Tanner Novel - Book 31

VENGEANCE - A Tanner Novel - Book 32

TARGET: TANNER - A Tanner Novel - Book 33

BLACK SHEEP - A Tanner Novel - Book 34

FLESH AND BLOOD - A Tanner Novel - Book 35

NEVER SEE IT COMING - A Tanner Novel - Book 36

MISSING - A Tanner Novel - Book 37

CONTENDER - A Tanner Novel - Book 38

TO SERVE AND PROTECT - A Tanner Novel - Book 39

STALKING HORSE - A Tanner Novel - Book 40

THE EVIL OF TWO LESSERS - A Tanner Novel - Book 41

SINS OF THE FATHER AND MOTHER - A Tanner Novel - Book 42

SOULLESS - A Tanner Novel - Book 43

The Young Guns Series in order

YOUNG GUNS
YOUNG GUNS 2 - SMOKE & MIRRORS
YOUNG GUNS 3 - BEYOND LIMITS
YOUNG GUNS 4 - RYKER'S RAIDERS
YOUNG GUNS 5 - ULTIMATE TRAINING
YOUNG GUNS 6 - CONTRACT TO KILL
YOUNG GUNS 7 - FIRST LOVE
YOUNG GUNS 8 - THE END OF THE BEGINNING

A Tanner Series in order

TANNER: YEAR ONE
TANNER: YEAR TWO
TANNER: YEAR THREE
TANNER: YEAR FOUR
TANNER: YEAR FIVE

The TAKEN! Series in order

TAKEN! - LOVE CONQUERS ALL - Book 1
TAKEN! - SECRETS & LIES - Book 2
TAKEN! - STALKER - Book 3
TAKEN! - BREAKOUT! - Book 4
TAKEN! - THE THIRTY-NINE - Book 5
TAKEN! - KIDNAPPING THE DEVIL - Book 6
TAKEN! - HIT SQUAD - Book 7
TAKEN! - MASQUERADE - Book 8

TAKEN! - SERIOUS BUSINESS - Book 9

TAKEN! - THE COUPLE THAT SLAYS TOGETHER - Book 10

TAKEN! - PUT ASUNDER - Book 11

TAKEN! - LIKE BOND, ONLY BETTER - Book 12

TAKEN! - MEDIEVAL - Book 13

TAKEN! - RISEN! - Book 14

TAKEN! - VACATION - Book 15

TAKEN! - MICHAEL - Book 16

TAKEN! - BEDEVILED - Book 17

TAKEN! - INTENTIONAL ACTS OF VIOLENCE - Book 18

TAKEN! - THE KING OF KILLERS – Book 19

TAKEN! - NO MORE MR. NICE GUY - Book 20 & the Series Finale

The MR. WHITE Series

PAST IMPERFECT - MR. WHITE - Book 1

HUNTED - MR. WHITE - Book 2

The BLUE STEELE Series in order

BLUE STEELE - BOUNTY HUNTER - Book 1

BLUE STEELE - BROKEN - Book 2

BLUE STEELE - VENGEANCE - Book 3

BLUE STEELE - THAT WHICH DOESN'T KILL ME - Book 4

BLUE STEELE - ON THE HUNT - Book 5

BLUE STEELE - PAST SINS - Book 6

BLUE STEELE - DADDY'S GIRL - Book 7 & the Series Finale

The CALIBER DETECTIVE AGENCY Series in order

CALIBER DETECTIVE AGENCY - GENERATIONS- Book 1

CALIBER DETECTIVE AGENCY - TEMPTATION- Book 2

CALIBER DETECTIVE AGENCY - A RANSOM PAID IN BLOOD- Book 3

CALIBER DETECTIVE AGENCY - MISSING- Book 4

CALIBER DETECTIVE AGENCY - DECEPTION- Book 5

CALIBER DETECTIVE AGENCY - CRUCIBLE- Book 6

CALIBER DETECTIVE AGENCY – LEGENDARY – Book 7

CALIBER DETECTIVE AGENCY – WE ARE GATHERED HERE TODAY - Book 8

CALIBER DETECTIVE AGENCY - MEANS, MOTIVE, and OPPORTUNITY - Book 9 & the Series Finale

THE TAKEN!/TANNER Series in order

THE CONTRACT: KILL JESSICA WHITE - Taken!/Tanner - Book 1

UNFINISHED BUSINESS – Taken!/Tanner – Book 2

THE ABDUCTION OF THOMAS LAWSON - Taken!/Tanner – Book 3

PREDATOR - Taken!/Tanner - Book 4

DETECTIVE PIERCE Series in order

MONSTERS - A Detective Pierce Novel - Book 1

DEMONS - A Detective Pierce Novel - Book 2

ANGELS - A Detective Pierce Novel - Book 3

THE OCEAN BEACH ISLAND Series in order

THE MANY AND THE ONE - Book 1

SINS & SECOND CHANES - Book 2

DRY ADULTERY, WET AMBITION - Book 3

OF TONGUE AND PEN - Book 4

ALL GOOD THINGS... - Book 5

LITTLE WHITE SINS - Book 6

THE LIGHT OF DARKNESS - Book 7

STERN ISLAND - Book 8 & the Series Finale

THE REVENGE Series in order

JOHNNY REVENGE - The Revenge Series - Book 1

THE APPOINTMENT KILLER - The Revenge Series - Book 2

AN I FOR AN I - The Revenge Series - Book 3

ALSO

THE EFFECT: Reality is changing!

THE FIX-IT MAN: A Tale of True Love and Revenge

DOUBLE OR NOTHING

PARKER & KNIGHT

REDEMPTION: Someone's taken her

DESOLATION LAKE

TIME TRAVEL TALES & OTHER SHORT STORIES

THE LIFE & DEATH OF CODY PARKER
Copyright © REMINGTON KANE, 2015
YEAR ZERO PUBLISHING

This book is a work of fiction. Names, characters, places and incidents either are products of the author's imagination or are used fictitiously.

Any resemblance to actual events or locales or persons, living or dead, is entirely coincidental.

All rights reserved. Except as permitted under the U.S. Copyright Act of 1976, no part of this publication may be reproduced, distributed or transmitted in any form or by any means, or stored in a database or retrieval system, without the prior written permission of the publisher.

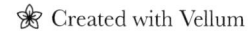

❀ Created with Vellum

Printed in Great Britain
by Amazon